Braving the Fire

Braving the Fire

John B. Severance

Clarion Books
New York

Clarion Books
a Houghton Mifflin Company imprint
215 Park Avenue South, New York, NY 10003
Copyright © 2002 by John B. Severance

The text was set in 11-point Sabon.
Book design by Sylvia Frezzolini Severance.

www.houghtonmifflinbooks.com

Printed in the USA.

Library of Congress Cataloging-in-Publication Data

Severance, John B.
  Braving the fire / by John B. Severance
      p. cm.
Summary: Jem joins the Union Army but is not sure of his motives
or what he hopes to accomplish, particularly since the Civil War
has divided his family and caused much violence and confusion in his life.
      ISBN 0-618-22999-X
1. United States—History—Civil War, 1861–1865—Juvenile fiction.
[1. United States—History—Civil War, 1861–1865—Fiction.] I. Title.
PZ7.S5153 Br 2002
[Fic]—dc21   2002003630

QUM 10 9 8 7 6 5 4 3 2 1

For my two brothers, Alex and Renny,
and for our sister, Tij,
in memory of our
Gaithersburg heritage

❧

It is only those who have neither fired a shot,
nor heard the shrieks and groans of the wounded,
who cry aloud for blood, more vengeance,
more desolation. War is hell.

—*General William Tecumseh Sherman*
U.S. Army
1879

Braving the Fire

Chapter One

LIKE THE WARNING RUMBLE OF distant thunder, the word "war" had slipped into the conversation again. The moment he heard it, Jem knew that another storm of bitter words was about to shatter the tranquility of supper. His appetite for the good food he had been smelling seemed to evaporate, but that would hardly matter, because by the end of the meal neither his father nor his grandfather would notice the uneaten food. During one of their arguments a treasured soup tureen had fallen off the top of the glass-fronted china cupboard, and they had barely paused for breath at the stunning crash.

At first, as they were pulling out their chairs to sit down, Jem had hoped that at least this one meal might be peaceful. The three bowed their heads while Granddad said grace. When he looked up, his bright hazel eyes and bushy gray mustache made him seem like the king of good cheer presiding at the head of the table. He had shed his suit jacket because of the hot summer weather, but his black woolen vest was fully buttoned, with a gold watch chain swagged across his trim waist. Jem sat on the side to Granddad's left. On the other side of the table Pa, gaunt and dark eyed, unfolded his napkin while making the offhand comment that inadvertently set off the verbal cloudburst.

"Our railroad surveyor left us to go and lay out track for the Army," he remarked in a conversational tone. "So with more of the directors gone and my medical leave from

Army duty almost up, the whole idea of a railroad link from Laurel through Gaithersburg has to be set aside for the rest of the war."

War, thought Jem grimly. Now Granddad's going to chime in.

"And who knows how long the war will go on?" said Granddad gruffly as he poured giblet gravy over his mashed potatoes. "Fellows over at the mill today were saying that fool Lincoln's likely to have to fire another general. Goes to show you, doesn't it? You can't count on a backwoods lawyer to know about running a war."

Is a city lawyer smarter? Jem wondered. Is a lawyer ignorant just because he's from the backwoods?

"He's a good enough lawyer to know the Constitution," said Pa, fervently, "and he means to save the Union."

"How's he going to save the Union if none of his generals can win battles for him and he has no choice but to fire them one after another? Then what good's his precious Constitution?"

"The Constitution's more important than any military personnel."

"Not if General Lee finally whips the Yankees good and proper, puts those Blue Bellies in their place."

"The Constitution's one of the greatest documents ever written."

"And you're a fool, Tom Bridwell!"

Jem gasped as though a bucket of cold water had been dumped on him. A fool? No sir! he thought. My pa's real smart. He can't be a fool.

"You raised me to think for myself, Father. I never would have thought you could raise a fool."

"If I say my own son's a fool, then that's what he is!"

shouted Granddad, slamming the table so hard the silverware jumped and the glasses clinked. "And I'm another one for failing to raise him to know what's right."

"I believe I know what's right."

"Freeing the slaves? You think that's right? You applaud those slick politicians in Washington telling the state of Maryland how we should live our lives? Oh yes. I know the Emancipation Proclamation doesn't apply to us border states, only to the Confederates, but that's just a sop to keep us in the Union. I bet that even now they're trying to figure a way to make us free our slaves. But I say if we want them to be free, that's our decision and no one else's business. Tom, have you bothered to imagine what a world of troubles emancipation will bring down on our heads? I say you're a fool for letting a bunch of Yankees up north do your thinking for you and letting them talk you into wearing their uniform and doing their dirty work for them.

"And while we're at it," continued Granddad, "I should point out that you'd just as soon reject your own way of life. If your mother had lived, she would have taught you some pride in the traditions to which you were born. But if my lovely Eveline were here now, you'd be breaking her heart just as you're breaking mine. A man who would cast out his own heritage is worse than a fool. I might as well come right out with it," said Granddad harshly. "Thomas Bridwell, you're a traitor."

Tears welled up in Jem's eyes as he watched his father slowly rise.

"I've been denounced in the church and in the tavern," said Pa, his voice trembling as he carefully placed his napkin on the dining table. "Some folks call me a moral monster, but I never thought to hear similar words from my own father." He strode out of the room and into the front parlor.

Jem stared at the dark shadows beyond the doorway. Then he shifted his blurred gaze to Granddad, hoping the tears wouldn't trickle down his cheeks. He knew, of course, that there was a war going on. *I'd have to be both deaf and stupid to miss it,* he thought, *but I sure wish we could just keep it out of the dining room. It always gets them riled up.* Jem's loyalty was stretched to the ripping point across the yawning canyon between his father and his grandfather. He loved them both.

THE BRIDWELL FARM NESTLED COMFORTABLY in the rolling hills of Gaithersburg, Maryland, eighteen miles northwest of Washington, D.C. Unlike the grand tobacco and cotton plantations of tidewater country near the seacoasts of Maryland, Virginia, the Carolinas, and Georgia, it did not have platoons of Africans to work in its few fields of corn and wheat. There were, however, seven adults and two small children living in the slave quarters on the farm. Four of the adults worked at cultivating the cash crops as well as hay for the livestock, but there was plenty of work left over for a healthy, husky fourteen-year-old boy like Jem. Always, there were the daily chores around the place, such as bringing firewood to the kitchen or, his least favorite, cleaning the hen house. At harvest times, when everyone was needed, Jem worked right alongside the four black field hands.

Pa had also done considerable labor on the farm before joining the Union Army and going off to war. Some people thought he was a bit eccentric, because many citizens of Gaithersburg, probably the majority, tended to sympathize with the Confederacy. After surviving a good number of battles, Pa was seriously wounded at Chancellorsville, Virginia.

He spent some weeks in a hospital and was then sent home to recuperate. Jem watched him and worried. Pa should have stayed in that hospital. He's so fired up about working the farm that he'll get beat right down and never have the strength to go on back to the war, he thought. Course, if he gets himself all worn out, he'll have to stay right here. At least I'll have my pa around.

HAVING PA AROUND SUITED JEM just fine on the morning after the latest supper battle. The two climbed into the loft of the barn to tidy up for the next harvest of hay.

"Already hot as a baker's oven," Pa said as they were starting the chore.

Then they settled down to the work in silence, not wanting to make extra talk that would lengthen their task. Also, if they breathed too much hayloft dust into their lungs, they would have coughing fits all night long. As he gathered loose hay with a wooden-toothed rake, Jem thought about last night's argument. It was not the first time the verbal battle had clouded the warm family feeling of a meal together. Jem wished he knew of a way to intercede, but he hadn't thought of one yet. He might as well shove his hand into a hornet's nest. That way he'd only be stung a thousand times. They'd have to listen to *him* doing the yelling. The repeated argument was an echo of the war that dominated the thoughts of everyone Jem knew in Gaithersburg. He guessed that people all over Montgomery County had to be up the same stump.

Last month the *Montgomery County Sentinel* had reported that way out in Mississippi a general named Ulysses Grant had captured a city called Vicksburg after a long siege. Also last month there had been a colossal battle up north at Gettysburg, Pennsylvania. Folks said it was twice as bloody as Antietam. September 1863, only a few weeks away, would be the first anniversary of that gory battle fought at Sharpsburg, Maryland, fifty miles up the road. Jem had heard someone at Ward and Fulks's General Store say that Antietam Creek had flowed pure blood. The combined casualty count for the two sides came to more than fifty thousand soldiers killed or wounded.

At the rate casualties were piling up, Jem was afraid the war wouldn't last long enough for him to get himself bloodied. Of course, he thought, maybe I don't want that kind of pain. Don't know as I could stand that much hurting. Never mind briar scratches, shin bruises, and splinters. They're nothing to write home about, but I guess I don't know about real pain. Still, the war's the biggest thing I ever heard of in my life. Keeping out of it might be kind of yellow.

PA'S SCAR, LIT BY THE afternoon sun on his pale shoulder, was a startling purple-crimson splash. As Jem stood on the creek bank, peeling off his own sweaty, work-stained clothes, he tried to imagine the horrendous pain that his father must have endured from that gruesome jagged blaze.

"Does it still hurt?" he asked.

"Some days," said Pa. "They say that by and by you forget pain. Maybe one day I'll forget the punch of that shot, but I'll always remember the agony the surgeon caused poking around with his bullet probe to dig it out. But that's enough of that, Jem-boy. Right now it's time for a swim."

The two splashed into the slow currents of Seneca Creek. Meanwhile the farm dog, a collie mutt named Teddy, sniffed along the shallows by the bank, his tail wagging like a furry flag among the bulrushes whenever he scared up a frog. Father and son sank up to their necks in the tepid water, soaking up relief from the day's various muggy labors under the glaring eye of the August sun. Pa preferred to avoid discussing anything to do with Chancellorsville, and Jem usually refrained from asking about it, but secretly he admired the wound his father had received in that battle. It was a permanent medal of honor.

The stream was more or less clear at this time of year, but the water level was low, and after paddling around in small circles a few times, Jem and Pa turned back toward the bank. When they were in chest-deep water, Pa whacked the surface playfully to splash a handful at his son. Jem sputtered and flailed both arms, splashing Pa back. For a minute or two they were caught in a miniature hurricane of water until both of them got to laughing so hard, their arms just flopped around, slapping the surface like wet ropes. They crawled out on the bank, and as soon as they stretched out on the trampled grass to dry off, Teddy came out of the creek to shake his waterlogged hide, spattering their bare skin with mud and water. When their ribs stopped heaving and they could breathe more easily, they stood up and got dressed. While they walked slowly up the path that ran alongside Big Meadow and up toward the farmhouse, Teddy zigzagged ahead of them as though scouting the land for intruders.

"Now, that was a treat," said Pa, slicking his damp hair back with his fingers. "I'll miss the little pleasures when I have to go back. Don't have many opportunities while on campaign."

"And when do you go, Pa?"

"Whenever I get my orders. I guess they'll be here in a day or two, Jem-boy. I've already got my promotion to major, and if I can carry a pitchfork, I can carry a weapon. Right soon I'll just have to go."

"I wish you didn't have to," said Jem.

"Me, too, but the Army will be wanting me back. They're desperate for experienced officers."

"Because you're all getting killed or wounded?" asked Jem.

"I guess that's part of it, but that leads to the problem of the poor quality of replacement troops. There's brokers in the cities who get paid to scrape up the lame, the halt, and the blind, even thieves out of the slums, and ship them off to the training camps. We veterans have to try and make real soldiers out of that sort of trash. And then there's those blasted bounty jumpers. Real scoundrels, they are."

"What are bounty jumpers?"

"Well, you see, folks who volunteer for the Army are paid a sum of money. And added to that, now that Lincoln has been forced to draft men for the Army, fellows who don't want to go are allowed to pay other fellows three hundred dollars to take their places. There's a lot of rascals will join up in one corps, get paid their bounty, and then desert so they can sign up with another unit and collect another bounty and keep on jumping until they get rich or get caught."

"And if they're caught?"

"They get shot."

THE GAMBREL ROOF OF THE grand old barn built by Granddad's daddy was the first building they could see as they approached the back of the farmhouse, ancient and sturdy, guardian of the farm's welfare. Next, squatting among the trees, the slave quarters came into sight, three unpainted one-room cabins, cobbled out of logs and slab wood from the sawmill, solid but crude. Two small, dark urchins, not yet old enough to work in the fields, sat in an open doorway, shelling peas into a chipped pottery bowl that had been made on the farm long ago by the deft hands of a now-forgotten slave. One of the children waved, and Jem and Pa waved back.

As they walked on, the white gable end of the old house came into view and their eyes were drawn to the fluttering of a lace curtain in the open window of a corner room on the second floor.

"That's the room where you were born," Pa said proudly.

"I know," said Jem uneasily, anticipating the thought that he guessed would come next.

"It's also where your ma died."

Wordlessly, Jem studied the sadness in his father's face.

"When your ma and I were married," said Pa, "they said she was the prettiest woman in Montgomery County, but I thought she was the prettiest in the whole state of Maryland."

"And you were the smartest man," Jem replied uncertainly, knowing ahead of time that his intended encouragement was likely to fail.

"And a year later my Blanche died."

Birthing me, thought Jem. Seemed like he always choked up when they got to this part. He wasn't sure why. Maybe it was because he had never had the chance to know his own mother. Maybe because Pa had lost the woman he loved. Could be for Ma herself. She binds Pa and me together, he thought, but sometimes it's like she makes a shadowy little space between us. He wondered if Pa held him to blame for Ma's death. Maybe he did, but all the cemeteries in the county had a lot of graves of women who had died giving birth to babies.

As they approached the back door, a dark skeleton with a white apron appeared on the porch. Clutching a wooden kitchen spoon in her clawlike hand, old Bertie looked as though she was made of weathered kindling wood, her face an ancient walnut topped by a soft summer cloud of white hair.

"Mist' Thomas," she said in her scratchy voice. "Don't mean no disrespect, but you and Mist' Little-James best get cleaned up and hurry on in there. Mist' Big-James is waitin' on you two. He says you should know when supper is served."

"And you think we should know, too, don't you Bertie," teased Pa. "Only you're too polite to say so."

"I ain't sayin' nothin' 'bout that," cackled Bertie. "'Deed I ain't."

Jem wasn't listening to the gentle banter. As he worked the handle of the backyard water pump, he was brooding about the evening ahead. Would there be another storm in the dining room? he wondered gloomily.

Chapter Two

∾

HANK DAWSON AND JEM BRIDWELL had been best friends for as long as they could remember. Two summers ago, in July 1861, after hearing of the First Battle of Bull Run in Virginia some twenty-five miles south of Gaithersburg, they had invented a game of Yank and Reb. Jem preferred to be the Yank because Pa was in the Union Army. Hank liked the role of Reb because it seemed more dramatic, but he would have cheerfully played the Yank if Jem had ever wanted to be the Reb. It soon became one of their regular activities. With sticks for guns, they skirmished along the banks of Seneca Creek whenever the fish weren't biting. In the fall they discovered even better terrain while walking to and from the one-room schoolhouse that had been built on an unused corner of the Desellum farm.

"BAM! You're dead," Jem would yell.

"No sir!" Hank called back. "You missed."

"How could I miss?"

"'Cause you're a lousy shot."

"Am not! You're dead. You just won't admit it."

In the winter months the game could be played only on the way home in the afternoons. On frosty mornings each boy set out for school with his hands thrust deep into his jacket pockets, kept warm by hot baked potatoes. Later, the cooled potatoes would be eaten for lunch.

SOMETIMES JEM WOULD PLAY HOOKY from his farm tasks to work on model boats, which he would launch in a quiet

11

backwater of Seneca Creek. Since the process didn't involve dramatic action, Hank's view of Jem's boat-building projects was not so genial as his attitude toward their mock battles between Yank and Reb.

"Kids' work!" said Hank one day.

"Kids couldn't make a boat like this," Jem replied, shifting the delicate model into the shaft of the midday sun streaming through the small window of the hayloft.

"I still can't figure why you waste your time on them," grumbled Hank, scratching one of his barn-door ears. "We could be down in Seneca Creek right now, swimming or catching a mess of sunnies for supper. But not our Jem. No sir. He'd rather be sitting in a dusty hayloft, messing with a toy boat."

"I guess I must have told you a hundred times, Hank. My boats aren't toys. They're models."

"Doesn't rightly matter what they are. I don't know why you fritter away so much time on them."

"Kind of takes my mind off the farm work. I got to pay close attention when I make a boat. I get to thinking so hard, I forget about the stink of cleaning out the hen house."

"I s'pose rigging up a fishing pole might do the same," said Hank, scratching his other ear. "And sitting on the bank waiting for a bite would sure beat splitting up a pile of kindling wood."

"I got to split the kindling anyway," said Jem. "Making boats gets me to forget about hating chores."

"I guess I'd want to do my own forgetting down at the creek."

"Well, I guess I'm not stopping you. Why don't you just go on down to the creek?"

"I believe I'll do that," said Hank, rising from his bed of

hay like a huge praying mantis. In one long bean-pole stride, he was at the ladder. He swung awkwardly down, the copper-colored thatch on his head disappearing last, leaving a swirl of dust glittering in the rays of sunlight.

Jem straightened the foremast and sat back to admire the boat. She was a replica of a flat-bottomed oyster boat, a long slender craft called a sharpie. Jem had seen such boats on the Potomac waterfront when Pa had taken him to Washington for a visit. If a sharpie skipper could have studied the model, he would have been astonished at the accurate details. Every bit of standing and running rigging to be found on an oyster boat had been re-created with Bertie's strongest button thread, including the spare anchor line coiled in the bow.

Jem was just tightening one of the shrouds on the mainmast when he heard a rattle outside. This time of day it would likely be Granddad's buggy. Then he heard footsteps below. A gritty voice filtered up through the floorboards.

"Come on down, Jemmy-boy. I know you're up there. Bertie told me you didn't finish your morning chores. Your pa used to hide there when he was ducking chores. Did it myself in my time," said Granddad, chuckling quietly.

"Yes sir," called Jem, as he carefully set the model on the beam above the loft window.

"Just think of her grouching, Jem-boy. She'll be complaining her old black body's too old for hauling firewood and where is Mist' Little-James at, anyway?"

"I was just putting my boat model away," said Jem as he clambered down the ladder.

"I believe you've been making boats so long now, they must be a sight better than any I ever showed you how to make when you were just a little shaver."

"You got to see this one, Granddad. She's an old-time Chesapeake oyster boat."

"You'll have to lower her down, Jem-boy. My old bones haven't been able to hike up that ladder since Teddy was a pup."

Standing on the barn floor, the old man seemed as grand as a lone chestnut tree in the middle of a meadow. When Jem swung off the ladder, he was surprised to notice that his own hazel eyes were almost on a level with Granddad's. The two smiled at each other and turned shoulder to shoulder to walk out of the barn, followed by Teddy, who had been snoozing in a pile of hay.

Outside, Solomon waited beside the buggy, his white-toothed grin gleaming brightly in the sunshine.

"Please give Old Belle a good rubdown, Solomon, and maybe an extra measure of feed," said Granddad. "I worked her pretty hard this morning. She deserves it."

"Yes, Mist' Big-James. I expect she does. 'Deed she does," Solomon crooned to the old mare as Jem and Grandpa headed toward the house. "This poor horse, she gets tired every day, just like Solomon here, doing the same old work, day in, day out."

"JEM-BOY, I MISS THOSE DAYS when you were just a little squirt and rode everywhere with me in the buggy. Do you remember?"

"Sure. When I rode in the buggy, I felt like I was grown up. Over to the mill and all around the village. Seemed like you knew just about everyone."

"Still do, Jemmy-boy. Still do, from old Mr. Desellum at the mill on down to the youngest clerk at Ward and Fulks's store. Although I can't say I'm too happy with Fulks himself since he raised his whiskey to eighty cents a gallon. I make it my business to know them all, and I make it my business to know the farm, too, Jem-boy. Just mind the times we used to ride around here together."

"I remember, Granddad. I remember going to the creek on an August afternoon so's Belle could get herself a drink of water. And while she rested, you showed me how to make a whistle out of a stick you cut from a wild cherry tree. Just slid that bark off the wood and cut the finger holes for the different notes. I guess you showed me lots of things, Granddad."

"And there's lots more to learn, Jem-boy. That's why you have to work on the place so's you know it as well as I do, from tending crops right down to doctoring sick animals."

As they crossed the backyard, Bertie's cracked voice came from the back porch.

"Mist' Little-James, where'd you get to? I declare, I like to broke my old back carrying firewood to cook for you. Good thing I ain't cooking on the open hearth no more. And you better be thankful, too, Mist' Little-James. Ever since Mist' Thomas brought home that newfangled wood stove seems like there's a lot less firewood to carry."

"Don't you worry about Jem," called Granddad. "He's been doing a job in the barn. It's all right now."

Bertie harrumphed, turned like a rickety skeleton, and wobbled back into the kitchen. She had been born on the farm and had looked after Jem ever since he could remember anyone taking care of him. She had been Pa's nurse, too, and she sometimes hinted she'd looked after Granddad but Jem didn't believe it. Besides, he couldn't imagine Granddad ever being a youngster. It seemed as though he must have been born ready to run the farm, gray mustache and all.

Bertie couldn't have been more than a girl herself back then. That was hard to imagine, too.

A FEW EVENINGS LATER, THE scent of pine needles that had baked all day in the sweltering sun of late summer drifted on the warm air of the night as Pa and Jem sat on the steps of the back porch. Out in the darkness the flat chirping of the katydids in the treetops was a scratchy orchestra singing of a season's passing.

"Every summer they scrape away at the same old argument," remarked Pa. "Katy did, Katy didn't."

"Katy did, Katy didn't," repeated Jem. "Yes she did. No she didn't. You can't help wondering if they might truly be talking."

"It'll never be the same again."

"You think that's what they're really saying?"

"Oh. No, Jem-boy, I wasn't minding the katydids anymore. They're only talking about this season's change. That's all they know. Next year their children will be singing the same old song. I was thinking about how the changes going on now are going to bring on a new way of life we never imagined a few years ago."

"Like the railroad link you and Mr. Clopper and Mr. Latrobe were working on before the war?"

"Well, yes. That's one tiny example, but it's going to be a lot bigger than that. About the time General Beauregard fired on Fort Sumter, I heard that some folks out west in Illinois and Iowa were planning to run a line clear to the Pacific coast. Mr. Lincoln was mixed up in it somehow. Before he was elected president, you know, he was a railroad lawyer with lots of important friends in the business, especially at the Chicago and Rock Island Line. If he hadn't got bogged down with this infernal war, he'd likely be working on that plan right now."

"I'd sure like to ride on a train," said Jem.

"After the war, I'm sure you will. It'll knock your breath out just keeping up with progress. But Jem-boy, tonight I wasn't thinking that far ahead. I was thinking about the war itself. I have to go back to it tomorrow."

"You're not scared, are you?" asked Jem.

They listened to the katydids for a long time. Finally, Pa spoke in a faraway kind of voice.

"Concerned, more like. Oh, scared of battle, yes. Any thinking person would have to be, but I'm concerned about right here. When the Confederacy is licked, I'll come home, if the Good Lord spares me, to a farm where Bertie and Solomon and Uncle Milford and even the field hands will be free. Most likely they won't even be here. It'll be just you and me and Granddad working the place by ourselves. Even if we get a hired man or two, I won't be able to spare so much as a minute for the railroad."

"Pa! Bertie would never leave us. Nor Solomon either."

"Maybe. Maybe not. You and I don't know what it feels like to be slaves. It's hard to imagine just what we'd do in their place. But the war will change all of our lives. Theirs and ours."

"I wish I could come with you."

"Now, why in blazes would you want to do a thing like that, Jem-boy?"

"For the glory, Pa."

"There's no glory in this war, son, nor in any other, I would imagine. It's a dirty, exhausting, bloody business."

"Exciting, too."

"Mostly not, I'd say. Be thankful you've got your work cut out for you here on the farm."

"Splitting kindling and hauling firewood's not exciting, Pa. And mucking out stables sure isn't. Especially mucking out stables. I'm not thankful for that. I hate it."

"Jem-boy, you'd be doing a lot of the same chores if you were in the Army, and a few new ones, too. Life's full of tasks you have to do even if you don't want to. Be glad you get to do yours in peace. And get ready to do a whole bunch more than you've ever done before."

THE NEXT MORNING PA WENT into the kitchen to say good-bye to Bertie. As he bent to kiss her, she gazed into his brown eyes and placed her dark, bony hands caressingly on each of his pale cheeks as though he were still the toddler she had taken care of years ago.

"Mist' Thomas," she said softly, "I know you got to go now. But you look out for yourself and come on back home. Y' hear?"

"I hear," whispered Pa.

With Jem hurrying along beside him, he strode through the house and out into the front yard, where Granddad was waiting. The two men shook hands woodenly.

"Father."

"Son."

Then Pa turned to his own son and wrapped his arms around him in a prolonged hug that was so tight, Jem could hardly find the strength to hug back.

"I still wish I could ride with you," said Jem, hoping the tears in his eyes would not spill out.

"I doubt you'd say that," replied Pa gently, "if you had any idea of what it's going to be like."

"Besides," Granddad added hoarsely, "you're needed right here."

The brass buttons on Pa's blue uniform glinted in the sunlight as he swung onto his horse. He looked smart and tall, as though he had nothing to worry about. Jem swelled up with pride. He thought if the war went on another year or so, he might join up anyway. They said if you were tall enough and strong enough, the recruiting officers never bothered to ask if you were eighteen. There just has to be some glory in it, Jem thought.

Pa sure seemed headed for glory. But when he rode down the dusty farm road that led to the Frederick Pike, you couldn't see all those bright buttons anymore, only a solitary soldier riding slowly along in one of the wheel ruts of a wagon track. Jem would learn you don't usually see one soldier all alone unless it's a dead one.

Chapter Three

THE NEXT DAY GRANDDAD SENT Jem out haying in Big Meadow with the four field hands and Bertie's cousin, who was called Uncle Milford for reasons no one could remember. The freshly cut hay smelled sweet and clean in the sun, but the work was hard. Getting hot and sweaty was normal for farm work, but Jem hated how the hay prickled his skin. The actual cutting was the hardest part. Farm work had made the palms of Jem's hands as tough as old leather. Nevertheless, each haying season he got at least one new blister from the scythe handle, and he couldn't rest when he felt like it. The lead field hand set the rhythm. Jem couldn't catch up and he couldn't lag behind. He had to keep pace with the crew as they moved single file across the field, slicing the hay into neat rows.

Just after the noon meal, the swinging reapers scared up a rabbit. The confused creature jumped up, zigzagged a couple of times, and then disappeared in the tall grass. The reapers never missed a beat.

"That rabbit, he's done gone," sang out the lead reaper.

"Onh-honh, he's done gone," said the next.

"'Deed he has. Done gone about his business," chuckled another.

"Yassir. Gone on about his business."

And so on back to the lead man. Then they would be quiet for a row or two before the chant began again.

All day long Solomon and Uncle Milford kept driving

wagons piled with carefully laid forkfuls of loose hay back to the barn. Each load was lifted whole into the hayloft by a giant iron claw on a block and tackle that was suspended from the roof peak. The forkfuls, called tumbles, would still be intact in winter, and when Jem went to feed the animals, he could count exactly how much hay was forked down to the livestock each day. He tallied the measures with care so the loft would not run out of hay before the arrival of warm weather.

As the sun reddened in the west, Solomon called to Jem, "This here's the last load, Mist' Little-James. I sure would like for you to drive it back to the barn so's I can ride with Uncle Milford. We got to talk some business."

THE FOLLOWING MORNING AT BREAKFAST, Granddad looked as though someone had nailed him to his chair.

"Tell me that again, Bertie."

"He's gone, Mist' Big-James. He done gone on about his business."

"His business is here on the farm," growled Granddad.

Jem sat staring at his flapjacks. Just before breakfast Granddad had sent him over to the barn to ask Solomon to hitch up Old Belle for an early ride into the village. Solomon wasn't there, so he had returned to the house to ask Granddad if he should run to Solomon's cabin and see if he was sick. He hadn't found Solomon anywhere.

"Some folks would say you're right about his business, Mist' Big-James," said Bertie, standing in the kitchen door with a platter of bacon in her hand. "Time was, Solomon would say so himself. But he's been thinking about his business a long time. You know he's not shiftless. You know that, Mist' Big-James, or you wouldn't have made him boss of the barn."

"I certainly would not have put him in charge of the barn if I thought he might run away."

"You know he didn't just run off like any old field hand," said Bertie. "He's been thinking and thinking, Mist' Big-James, and come to think his business is changing. He got to thinking if the freedom time's coming, he can't just lay around and wait for it. He believes he's got to go and help fight for that freedom. Solomon's gone to the Army."

A WEEK AFTER THE DISRUPTED breakfast, Granddad and Jem stood side by side and gazed into a small, plain framed mirror in Granddad's bedroom.

"Jem-boy, I want you to think about taking on new responsibilities," Granddad said to their reflections.

The mirror hung on swivels attached to the lathe-turned sticks set in the top of the low shaving stand that stood on top of Granddad's bureau. The elegant little cabinet was the only piece of furniture Jem had ever truly admired. The main part was no more than eight inches tall and held a bellied drawer with two glass knobs. That was for the shaving things. The narrower flanking sections were an inch or two higher, and each of them had two little drawers in which Granddad stored such items as handkerchiefs, studs, cuff links, and sometimes his gold pocket watch and chain.

"Your grandmother Eveline gave this to me when we were married, the day she took the name Bridwell," said Granddad, fingering one of the glass knobs. "When I've passed on, I want you to have it." In the mirror their hazel eyes were identical in color, but that was the only resemblance. Granddad had his wide gray bush of a mustache and a sandpaper chin. Jem had freckled cheeks and the delicate, thin fur of a budding beard alongside each ear.

"It's a good thing you're just about grown," said Granddad, turning to face Jem, "because I'm giving you a man's responsibility. I want you to look after the farm while I'm gone."

"Granddad!" said Jem, feeling an inner fright he hoped didn't show. "Pa's already in the Army. You don't need to go."

"Put your mind at rest, Jem-boy. If your pa and I were both in this war, we'd stand some chance of shooting each other. You know if I went, I'd have to join up with the Confederates. No, no, I'm just going away a little while to look for supplies, maybe some barrels of flour and a couple of hogs."

"But Granddad, we've still got a barrel and a half from the Gaithersburg mill, and the smokehouse is busting with hams and two sides of bacon. Plenty to last."

"Over at Fulks's store yesterday, they were saying Confederate foragers have crossed the Potomac again. You know they've come across to Rockville more than once for horses. I'm thinking we'll need to hide a spare supply in the woods. Between them and the Union boys, who've already been through and might come back, we could starve to death right here on the farm."

"But they couldn't take goods and animals from you," Jem protested. "Confederates wouldn't take property away from Confederates."

"And how would they be sure I am a Confederate? Maryland's not even in the Confederacy. It's a border state, and I could be for either side. Even if they took me at my word, they might not care. Or they might say it's my duty to give supplies to the troops. War is never fair, and you can't argue with a bunch of men carrying guns. Another thing. I have to see if I can hire a hand to look after the barn and livestock. That's if I can find a healthy man who hasn't gone to war."

"You said I'm getting to be a man," said Jem. "I could do the job." Jem could hardly believe he was asking for more chores.

"You're already helping like a man, Jem-boy, and you'll be doing two men's work before this war is over. We'll have a hard time just to keep going if the field hands take after Solomon. I'm right surprised they haven't run off already. Mr. Lincoln's confounded Emancipation Proclamation doesn't apply to border states, but legal notions wouldn't stop them. Those hands will just pick up and go if they get their minds set on it. Pray to the Lord Bertie stays in the kitchen—not that she has anywhere else to go, poor old soul.

"And talking about being a man, there's more I have to tell you." Granddad pulled open the left lower drawer of the shaving stand. He lifted two handkerchiefs and revealed four ten-dollar gold pieces nested in a corner of the bottom. "I put them here for what you might call a calamity fund. I guess the situation qualifies. Forty dollars might not be a fortune, but it's a right good sum. If something happens to me, that's for you to do the best you can. If the Lord spares me, I'll be back in two days."

JEM WAS WORRIED AS THEY walked out to the barn to hitch the oldest team of horses to the oldest wagon. He felt a tightly knotted ball in the middle of his belly. Mostly he was thinking about Pa. Maybe he'd done the right thing after all. Jem did not dare to suggest this to Granddad. That would only start a tirade about Pa being a fool. But in contrast to the drama of war, life on the farm was looking more than just a little bit boring. It was getting harder and somewhat worrisome. And wherever Pa was, he must be having a grand time rolling up the glory. Jem wished he were riding with Pa. Of course, Pa would never permit such a thing, but staying at home was beginning to seem cowardly. I wonder if I'll ever find a way to get into the war before it's all over, Jem mused.

They rode together in the creaking wagon as far as the Frederick Pike. Jem dropped off into the dusty road and said good-bye to Granddad.

"Good-bye, Jemmy-boy," said Granddad. "You keep after those rats in the corncrib. I believe they've been getting a little uppity since Solomon left."

Granddad sounded cheerful, but he looked mighty weary, and so did the horses plodding up the lonely road. Jem didn't go back to the house. He walked slowly down to Seneca Creek to do some hard thinking. He found Hank sitting on the bank with his fishing pole lying idle in the grass beside him.

"No fish biting," grumbled Hank. "Guess it's already too hot for them. Must be laying low on the bottom. Might stir them up a little if we was to go in swimming."

They did that, but it seemed as though their hearts weren't truly in it. There was none of the usual whooping and howling. Hank was big on howling. The more he did it, the more Jem laughed, and the louder Jem laughed, the more Hank howled. They couldn't quit until their ribs ached. But now they just kind of paddled around awhile and then flopped down on the bank to dry in the sunshine.

"Won't be much more of this," said Jem. "Seems like every time I turn around, there's more chores for me to get onto."

"Ma started giving me more chores three years ago, after

my pa died," said Hank. "Lately she's got a bunch of new ones every day. I swear she sits up nights thinking up chores no one ever heard of before."

"Well, now I get to think up my own chores. Granddad went away this morning. Before he left, he told me I had to look after the place myself."

"Jehosaphat!" said Hank, sitting straight up. "Your old granddad went off to the war?"

"No. I don't believe he'd ever do that. It's only for two days, he said, but there's bound to be even more work when he gets back. There already is since our barn hand ran away."

"Solomon?" asked Hank. "Well, who'd believe it? I always thought he was almost part of your family."

"It's enough to make me think about running off myself, and I *am* part of the family."

"I'd do it, Jem. Oh yeah. I'll do it if you'll do it. Think of the glory." Hank jumped up, his red hair glowing like a grass fire in the sunlight. "We'll ride with Jeb Stuart's cavalry, killing Yankees left and right." He slashed at some bushes with a stick. "It'll be grand, and we'll never have to do farm work again. That will be grandest of all."

"I don't know, Hank," Jem said slowly. "Leaving the farm is one thing, but I figure I'd have to go into the Union Army, like my pa. I know most folks in Gaithersburg favor the Confederacy, but he makes right good sense about preserving the Union. I guess I'd rather ride with Pa than with Jeb Stuart. My granddad's Confederate, though, and he'd sure enough try to stop me."

"He doesn't have to know about it."

"He'll know after I'm gone. He'd start calling me a fool just like he calls my pa. And that's his own son."

"After you're gone, there's nothing your granddad can do about it." Hank's eyes were sparkling like Christmas. "I guess I'd just as soon be a Blue Belly Yank as a Gray Back Reb. Why, we even met a few good Yanks last summer when we rode Old Belle down to Cabin John Creek looking for better fishing. Remember? Even wearing Federal uniforms, there'd likely be enough glory to go around. Getting away from chores for good is the main thing. Come on, Jem. Let's go. Come on, boy. Where's your spunk?"

"I got plenty of spunk, Hank. I just got to figure out where to use it. Saving the Union makes sense to me even if it means freeing the slaves. And maybe they should be free. My pa got me to thinking about those things a lot. But he wouldn't want me to go, and anyway I'd be letting my granddad down if I did. But if I stay home with Granddad, I miss out on the glory. Seems like I'm stuck in a real bind."

"Jem-boy, can't you see it? Glory is what it's all about. We'll be heroes when we come home. We'll be famous. Folks'll cheer us all around town. They'll look up to us. Ask us for advice. Elect us mayor. Maybe we'll even get rich."

"I know all that, Hank. I guess I just got to think about it some."

"Well, Jem-boy," said Hank, picking up his fishing pole, "I sure do hope the Battle of Gettysburg wasn't our last chance. Old General Bobby Lee's already taken his army of Rebs back to Virginia. The war might be over and done with before you make up your mind."

Chapter Four

WHEN JEM GOT HOME, BERTIE was pumping water at the soapstone kitchen sink and a stockpot was simmering on the wood stove. He reached carefully around the pot to pick up the kettle of hot water that was sitting on the back of the stove.

"Where you going with hot water?" barked Bertie.

"Going to wash," mumbled Jem.

"Land sakes, child, you don't need your washing water to be hot unless it's for your Saturday night bath!"

"I'm not a child anymore, Bertie, and I've got to go and shave."

"Well! I declare! Mister Big Man! Regular water ain't good enough for him. 'Deed no. This child's no child. Just got to have hot water for his precious whiskers."

Jem scuttled out of the kitchen, hoping Bertie would stop her clucking, but as he climbed the back stairs, her scratchy voice pursued him. "Maybe Mister Big Man's going to remember to fetch some firewood so's old Bertie can make up some more hot water. Or maybe he'll get his daddy's old squirrel gun and shoot them bodacious rats in the corncrib so's my poor chickens won't be ate out of house and home."

He turned at the top of the stairs, entered the silence of Granddad's room, and set the kettle by the washbasin. He opened the center drawer of the little shaving stand and took out the straight razor, the bowl of soap, and the lathering brush. He lined them all in a row on the bureau. Then he reached for the mirror and tilted it to an angle that would reflect his face.

Jee-hos-a-PHAT! There was a second face in the mirror, one Jem had never seen before, just behind his right shoulder. Its cold eyes seemed to freeze him as solid as the ice pond in January. There was a nose like a turkey buzzard's and a bush of whiskers as prickly looking as a barberry hedge. But none of that was especially alarming. It was the eyes. They were the lightest, chilliest blue Jem had ever seen, and so flat he couldn't read the man. It was like trying to read the eyes of some kind of hawk or vulture.

Jem stared at the mirror as if staring hard enough would make the face fade away like a puff of smoke from Uncle Milford's corncob pipe. Instead, the face grew larger and broke into a gap-toothed grin. A red claw clutched Jem's shoulder and hauled him right around.

"Say, Ezra," croaked the scrawny man. "Lookit what we got here."

Another bearded scarecrow drifted silently from the shadows in the hall and stopped in the doorway. "Looks like a young sprout fixing to skin some fuzz off the peach," said Ezra.

"Yeah. Seems we got here just in time to show him there's no need of that. The Good Lord meant for something to grow on a man's chin."

The first man held a pistol in one hand and a gunny-sack in the other. The second cradled a long rifle in the crook of his elbow, and he also carried a sack. Old Turkey Buzzard stuck the pistol in his belt and scooped two matching silver-backed hairbrushes off the bureau. Looking closer, Jem saw that what he had thought was an old sack was actually a lace-edged pillowcase that had belonged to his mother. Without a thought he made a grab for the brushes.

"Don'tcha move," said Turkey Buzzard, pulling out his pistol.

For the second time in a minute Jem froze. He stood up against the bureau like a green stalk of feed corn and watched as Ezra banged Grandpa's wardrobe open and pawed through the shelves and the clothes rack. The Sunday-best suit slid off its hanger into a dark heap on the floor. Jem hoped they wouldn't notice the shaving stand behind him. If they got to pulling out the little drawers, the gold pieces were gone for sure.

"Fire!" came a shout from downstairs.

The cry was echoed by strange voices in other parts of the house.

"Fire!"

"FIRE!"

Ezra and Turkey Buzzard vanished as abruptly as they had appeared. Jem's knees suddenly felt like crab-apple jelly. He wobbled to a chair, collapsed, and then jumped up again almost immediately. There was a whiff of smoke in the air. Jem ran for the back stairs but halted at the top step. There seemed to be a loud set-to going on in the kitchen below. Bertie's cracked voice was at full volume along with a man's gruff voice. Teddy was growling and yapping. Jem thought a moment and decided he wouldn't be helping much if he dropped straight into the hullabaloo. He figured it would be better to go down the front stairs, outside, around the house, and mosey in the back door sort of casually. At least he wouldn't get trapped, and maybe he could help Bertie get loose from the fracas.

Jem tore back through the upstairs hall, took a quick detour through Granddad's room, and grabbed the shaving stand on the run. If the house were to burn, at least the little shaving stand would be saved and so would the money in it. Jem took the front stairs like a jackrabbit, shot out the door, and ran around to the backyard and smack into a bunch of raggedy men. Some were standing like scarecrows and some were seated on slat-ribbed horses. They were all staring at the barn as it burned. The loft full of hay must have speeded things along. The results of all those hard days of scything were now big black clouds of smoke just rolling up into the blue sky. The roof and most of the siding were already gone. Along with my boat model, thought Jem. The heavy timbers of the frame looked like a fiery skeleton.

There was no way to fight such a blaze, but the four field hands were feverishly hauling full and dripping buckets from the watering trough to the slave cabin closest to the doomed barn. So far they had managed to keep the thin cedar shingles of the roof well soaked, so sparks could not set it on fire. Uncle Milford was teetering on the ridge pole of the next cabin, struggling to spread wet blankets over the roof. The last cabin and the main house seemed safe for the moment.

"What the sam hill do you folks think you're doing?" Jem screamed.

A hand gripped his elbow tight as a blacksmith's pincers. It was Ezra again. There was a gray-looking man sitting in Granddad's buggy. His tattered tunic had a few tarnished metal buttons, as though it might once have been part of a military uniform. Next to him, on the seat, were a side of bacon and two smoked hams. Six of Bertie's fattest hens dangled over the back, tied to the buggy by their feet.

"You'd rob all this from us? And how are we gonna run the farm with the barn in ashes? Think you're soldiers? You're ANIMALS! Pack of mean hounds! WILD DOGS!" Jem had never yelled at grown men before. He had lost his head.

"There's times we might agree, son," said the man in the buggy. His voice was soft and creaky, as though there wasn't much left of him. "We didn't intend to set fire to the barn, but we certainly meant to take the food and livestock. We need them."

It was then Jem noticed that three of the men were each leading a cow, and two more held the halters of the farm's two best horses.

"But my grandfather's Confederate," Jem gasped. "If he could be here now, he'd be proud to swear to it. You can't take from him. You're stealing."

"We'd rather call it 'requisitioning,'" said the weary leader, holding out a piece of crumpled paper. "This voucher lists all the supplies and livestock we've taken. The government in Richmond will reimburse you after the war."

"And what about the barn?"

"That was an accident. Someone must have ignored my orders prohibiting smoking. Maybe dropped a lit cigar. You could put in a claim, but there's not much we can do about it right now."

"But what the devil are we going to live on until the war is over? It's just not fair."

"There's not much in war that is fair, son. You'd best come on with us. We can always use another soldier. There's nothing here for you now."

"You think I'd go with robbers and vandals? You tore our place apart, and I guess you'd expect me to help you tear others apart."

"Makes no difference what you think of us. Fact is, young feller, there's no safety here. Not for you. Not for anyone else. This fire's got to be noticed in Emory Grove, maybe even as far as Rockville, and there might be Union troops in the area. And there's always marauders who don't rightly belong to anyone's army. Just loot and kill for the sport of it. Corporal Burke, bring this young man one of his horses. Men, let's move on toward the river. We have no time to waste."

Jem tried to holler, but the sound stuck in his throat. He broke loose from Ezra, scurried around the buggy, and ran full tilt into the tall corn, feeling like a scared rabbit. He ran down the rows until he could run no more and just had to flop down. When he finally stopped heaving for breath, he noticed his grandfather's shaving stand on the ground beside him. The tilted mirror was reflecting the pink clouds that were floating above the setting sun.

As Jem walked back to the farmhouse, he saw that the kitchen lamps were lit. It cheered him a little to be coming home to Bertie, but he was also worried, because he had run off without thinking about her. Now he was afraid of what the foragers might have done to her. He climbed the back porch steps and went into the kitchen.

Bertie was there, crouched at the far side of the stove. With both hands she held her biggest frying pan high above her head. "Praise the Lord, it's you, Mist' Little-James." She sighed and hung the skillet back on its hook. "I feared you might be one of them robber men again. And praise the Lord, you come back! I thought sure they up and took you away, and how was I going to explain that to your granddaddy when he come home?"

But Granddad didn't come home. A week and a half after the barn burned, Jem and Uncle Milford sat in the kitchen while Bertie was cooking supper.

"Going to have to cut back some," said Uncle Milford. "Can't work this farm since all the field hands run off. I expect I'd go, too, was I young enough. Then I'd surely be goin' to the war, but these old bones wouldn't stand for no fightin'. 'Deed they wouldn't."

"I believe I might go," said Jem casually, as though he were thinking of going swimming in the creek. He didn't feel casual, though. He was startled at his own words, and his insides knotted up.

"I heard there's plenty of lads younger than you in the Army," said Uncle Milford. "You're strong and big for your age from working on the farm. No farm for you to work now, Mist' James."

"Hear you talk!" cried Bertie, flinging a long-handled spoon into the sink and planting her hands on her bony hips. "Milford, you just hush your mouth! What kind of notions you carryin' around in that head of yours? Mist' Thomas and Mist' Big-James gone the Lord knows where, might be no one alive to run the farm when the war's finished and done."

"I guess I wouldn't mind getting back at them for the barn and all," muttered Jem.

"I declare! Ain't nobody talking sense around here," shouted Bertie. "Nobody! You hear me? Child, you don't even know if they was real Rebels. They let on they was, but there's lots of mean folks running around just looking out for what they can get."

"I guess they were real enough, Bertie. I know Granddad said he'd only be gone two days and here it is a week and then some, but you know how he loves this place. Soon enough he'll be back to look after it, and after you and Uncle Milford. Rebs won't get you."

"You getting yourself killed won't please him none, Mist' Little-James. And you know was he here, he wouldn't ever let you go."

Uncle Milford shifted in his chair. "Was I young, I believe I'd want to get in a few licks for freedom."

"Your own freedom," said Bertie. "Mist' Little-James, he's already born free. No need for him to die before the Good Lord's got a long white robe all cleaned up and fresh for him."

JEM WONDERED IF PA WOULD see things a little differently now if he knew the barn had been burned to the ground and the farm pretty well ruined. Stretched out on his bed, he stared into the darkness and considered how much he was really needed on the farm. After a while he rolled over and stared out the window at the eerie silver-gold fringe around the edges of a cloud that was blocking the full moon and pondered going to war. For very different reasons, both Granddad and Pa wouldn't want him to go. But when do I start thinking for myself? Jem asked the night sky.

He would have to talk it through with Hank. For years the two had been like brothers, squabbling sometimes but also listening to each other.

IN THE MORNING JEM FOUND Hank fishing from the bank of the creek.

"They're biting like they missed their breakfast," said Hank. "Where's your pole?"

"Can't fish. I'm thinking about joining up."

"Again?" said Hank as he yanked a small glittering sunny out of the water and dropped it flapping on the bank. "We been all over it. What's left to be thinking about? You think too. much."

"I think I might be ready to go."

"Well, jumping juniper! I'd about given up on you. I was beginning to think I might just have to pack up and go it alone. Wouldn't have been half the fun without you, Jem-boy. So I waited. Figured you'd likely come around. You never were a gen-u-ine scaredy-cat. But you just about wore me out with your sittin' on the fence so long."

"I told you, Hank. I had to think some. Still do. Maybe I was waiting on my granddad."

"Your granddad wasn't fixing to buy you a fast horse to ride away on. Mostly he would have tried to cramp your style."

"Well, don't you think I know that? Just didn't seem right to skin out of here behind his back."

"Jem-boy, didn't you ever think maybe he up and joined the Confeds? Could be he skinned out behind your back."

"He wouldn't do a thing like that without saying so, same as I wouldn't do it to him. Besides, when he left, he outright said he wasn't going to the Army. If he'd known I was going, it would have made him madder than a wet hen, but I wanted to face up to him."

"But now you don't have to," hooted Hank. "Come on, boy. What are you waiting for? Get back home and pack your satchel. I'll meet you out on the pike. Maybe we can hitch a ride on a wagon and be in Washington before sundown. There's Union camps just across the river in Virginia. Hallelujah! Glory, here we come!"

JEM STOOD BEHIND THE RICKETY rocker in the kitchen, waiting for Bertie to finish sewing a button on his spare shirt. He thought it was strange how sure he was now. It was like the sun coming out after a summer storm. He knew he was ready to leave. He didn't know why he was ready. He just knew he was on his way.

Maybe it was like Pa said. Preserve the Union. Maybe it was for Solomon and Uncle Milford and especially for Bertie, because she couldn't fight for her own freedom. Maybe it was a chance to make something of himself in a way that he never could staying on the farm. Granddad wouldn't want him joining the Yankees, but Jem had to make up his own mind now, and the farm was hardly a going concern. Maybe he could even find Pa and ride with him if he didn't send him home again. Preserving the Union, freeing the slaves, riding with Pa all got mixed together like something worth standing up for. He wanted to think that Granddad would be proud that his grandson had acted like a man.

"Glory be, child," said Bertie. "I see you're going to go and do whatever you've a mind to do just like any man. Stubborn as a mule, that's a man. I don't believe the Good Lord Himself could change a man's ways. You just go on about your business, Mist' Little-James. Go on about your business."

Chapter Five

"HAYFOOT! STRAWFOOT! HAYFOOT! STRAWFOOT! HAY. Straw. Hay. Straw. Hay . . . Hay . . . Hay . . . Pick up them feet now! Look smart! That's if you can, you ignorant clover kickers. Move it! Hay! Straw! Hay! Straw!"

Sergeant Snyder was from Baltimore. He believed that all Union recruits and draftees who were sent to Camp Cass in Arlington, Virginia, were country hicks who couldn't be trusted to know left from right. He had each new company tie blades of feed hay on their left ankles and blades of threshed straw on the right. As a city dweller himself, Snyder might have had difficulty telling hay from straw, but he figured that with his novel system, the assortment of country lads in his care could learn to march. This made it rather confusing for the city boys from the slums of Baltimore, but somehow most new soldiers learned left from right before they left Camp Cass for the battlefields of Virginia.

"Compan-ee, halt! . . . Straw-aw face!" Snyder squinted at the mismatched-looking ranks of soldiers in the noon sun. Their dusty uniforms were streaked and patched with stains of sweat. "You might think you're soldiers!" yelled the sergeant. "I'm here to tell you that you ain't! Not by a long shot! But when I get through with you greenhorns, you might at least look like soldiers even if you ain't. . . . What's that? Did I hear a complaint?" Sergeant Snyder stomped up to the front rank until the tip of his nose almost touched Hank's. "You got a gripe, Hayseed?"

"No sir," said Hank, staring back into Snyder's harsh dark eyes.

"You said SOMETHING."

"Yes sir. I said soldiers could stand a drop of water now and then."

"Soldier, didn't I just get through telling you yokels you ain't soldiers yet?"

"Yes sir."

"That's right, soldier! And do you know when you will be soldiers?"

"Another month, sir?"

"Wrong, soldier. You couldn't be more wrong. But then a hayseed's got so much chicken feathers between the ears, he's bound to be wrong no matter what. I'll tell you when you'll be soldiers! You'll be soldiers when I say you're soldiers! And until I say you're soldiers, I'll decide when and where you can stop for a drink of water." Snyder glared up and down the ranks. . . . "Hay-y face! . . . Forward march!"

The bedraggled company marched unsteadily off across the parched parade ground. Then they marched back again. They marched all afternoon to the yapping sound of Sergeant Snyder's insults. They paused only once, when a man fainted and had to be dragged off the field. Then they closed ranks and marched until sundown.

"Someday you'll thank me for this!" yelled Snyder, squinting into the red rays of the setting sun. "It's called discipline, and wherever you fight, you'll remember and you'll thank me." He dismissed them, and the company straggled away to the barracks.

"Thank him for what?" Hank asked hoarsely. "For sore backs and scratchy eyes? For blisters on our feet and dust in our gullets? When does the glory begin? That's what I'd like to know. We didn't join the Army to be pushed around and marched around and treated like a bunch of pea-brained jackasses."

"I guess the sergeant is one mean cuss for sure," said Jem, "but it seems like he's the only one who's going to teach us soldiering."

"Call this soldiering?" asked Hank. "Not on your auntie's washtub. This is more like prison. More like torture, I guess. I don't believe Fatty Rat's Eyes Snyder knows beans about real soldiering. And speaking about beans, how do you like the mushy ones we been getting with that slimy salt pork they been feeding us every ding-dong day? Hay, straw, blisters, dust, soggy beans, and green pork. That's gonna turn us into soldiers? What're soldiers supposed to be doing besides chasing Rebs around the countryside and shooting them now and then? Be more like hunting jackrabbits, and we already know more about that than Rat's Eyes ever will in a million years. Maybe, Jem-boy, maybe he's afraid of real soldiering."

THE BROTHERLY BOND THAT JEM and Hank had built over years back in Gaithersburg seemed to be growing even stronger in Camp Cass. This was definitely to their advantage when they had to deal with Samson Stiles. Samson wasn't his real name. He had been given it in honor of the bulging biceps he had developed in his peacetime trade of blacksmith.

Samson liked to "test" all young recruits who were smaller than he was. He said he wanted to be sure that anyone going into battle alongside him had the grit to fight. One evening, on his way to the latrine, Jem happened to bump into Stiles.

"Got to see if you know how to defend yourself like a man," growled the bully, dancing lightly on his toes. "Course you ain't rightly a man yet, are you? But you got to learn sometime." He gave Jem an open-handed slap on the left ear that made the inside of his head ring.

"This might be a good time for you to leave," said Hank, as he came out of the latrine. "Yes, I'm sure it is. Right now. You hear?"

The bully stopped, lurched slightly, and put his hands on his hips. "This here ain't none of your concern."

"I guess I can decide that for myself," said Hank, stopping just half a foot from the swaying giant. He sniffed and continued, "Especially with a galoot as drunk as you are."

"Just a couple of spring chickens," sneered the bully. "I could lick you both at the same time with my best hand tied behind my back."

"Supposing you was sober, you'd see you wouldn't even want to try," said Hank very quietly.

The big fellow seemed to swell with anger. Then he laughed. "Wouldn't want to waste my time whipping pullets," he said, and walked unsteadily away.

Hank winked at Jem and grinned. Jem winked back uncertainly.

"I don't know, Hank. I guess we're not soldiers yet."

"Close enough, Jem-boy."

"Well, maybe we're not men either."

"Shoot. We got to be men just by running away from Gaithersburg and not running back first time we got a little scared. Say, Jem, you're not fixing to run home now, are you?"

"Well, no," said Jem. "Never even thought of it. And anyway, I'd be shot for a deserter. I was just thinking it's a good thing you came along. I'll never be man enough to take on someone the size of Samson."

"His saying you're not a man doesn't make it so. You got more spunk, Jem. You know beating up folks like Samson's not all there is to being a man."

"But I'm not sure what is. You tell me, Hank, since you're so all-fired sure."

"You got me, Jem-boy. I'm not so all-fired sure as you think. I can't tell you for certain what makes a man a man. But I can sure tell you some things that don't."

Word got around. They were never bullied again, not by Samson Stiles or anyone else, not even the rough-cut professional bounty jumpers who had signed on for cash rewards. These thieves and drifters made everyone's life miserable until they found opportunities to disappear and sign on with another corps. Even though the more shifty types in camp now left Hank and Jem alone, the boys managed to get into a few other scrapes. Usually the incidents were their own fault, such as the time they slipped a mixture of gravel and mule dung into Sergeant Snyder's boots.

"Ooh-ow!" exclaimed Jem one evening as he examined his blistered feet. "I wish we could put something in Snyder's boots to make his feet as sore as ours."

"Yeah," said Hank, looking at his own red toes. "I'd like to see Fatty Rat's Eyes's all crippled up like an old man's."

The vision of Sergeant Snyder hobbling around the camp made them hoot with laughter. They started limping and hopping, causing the men nearby to stare at them. When Jem and Hank got so overcome with the joke that they rolled on the ground, the men shook their heads and went back to examining their own blisters.

"This is it," said Hank, sitting up suddenly. "This is the night. I heard Fatty Rat talking to a couple of other sergeants about a poker game tonight. You know how liquored up they all get at those games. When Snyder crawls under his blanket, he'll be snoring in a minute, and even the howling hounds of Hell couldn't wake him until reveille. We're gonna get him tonight, Jem-boy. This is it!"

IN THE MORNING THE SERGEANT had the whole company on the parade ground almost before the echoes of the reveille bugle call died away in the hills.

"Which one of you knotheads diddled my boots?" he yelled, as red in the face as an old tom turkey. He looked like a turkey, too, as he strutted and gobbled in front of the ranks. His eyes seemed ready to pop out of his head. "You'll step up and take your punishment like a man!"

There was silence on the field except for the flag flapping in the brisk morning breeze.

"Step up and 'fess up or the whole company will march till sundown without a break and you'll turn in without supper."

There was a hoarse whisper from the ranks behind Jem. "We heard you boys talkin' 'bout it," rasped Samson Stiles. "You let him march us till sundown, and your lives ain't worth a pig's whistle in a high wind."

It seemed just plain foolish to take on all the bullies in Camp Cass, so Jem and Hank confessed. The sergeant ordered two large, empty pork barrels rolled onto the parade ground and upended. The two boys were forced to stand for hours on the rims of the open barrels. When they had the time, most of the rest of the company lounged in front of them, jeering and joking and hoping to see the unhappy lads tumble down inside.

Shortly before sunset Sergeant Snyder had them stand at attention facing two wooden cracker crates. He seated himself on one and had his supper served on the other.

"Discipline," said Snyder between bites of stringy salt pork. "That's what it's all about. Discipline." He slurped some greasy-looking bean soup and wiped his mouth on the sleeve of his shirt. "You hear me? Discipline! And by grab, you're gonna thank me for it."

It was a typical Army meal, with a large serving of beans, but the sergeant carried on as though he were stuffing his pudgy face with a Sunday roast and all the trimmings. To Jem and Hank, headed for bed with empty stomachs, it seemed as though it just might have been a holiday feast.

"Discipline," grunted Hank when they were back in the barracks. "Supposed to thank him for it. So where's your manners, Jem?"

"I don't know but what some kinds of manners could buy us another peck of trouble. Best keep our mouths shut. But Hank, I guess we had us some fun. Isn't that what we wanted?"

"Too big a price on it for fun," said Hank, rubbing the toes of his left foot. "Especially now we're getting nearer to the war."

THE WAR SEEMED HARD TO find. When training was over, they were sent farther into Virginia as replacement troops for the Army of the Potomac. They saw very few Rebels along the way. Once Samson shot a lone sharpshooter out of an apple tree by an abandoned farmhouse. Another time a train loaded with Confederate prisoners rolled slowly by while the Union boys waited on a muddy road.

Shortly after Thanksgiving, an old holiday recently

revived by President Lincoln, Jem and Hank were re-assigned. They reported to the headquarters of Brigadier General Francis C. Barlow, who commanded a division of the Second Corps under the celebrated General Winfield S. Hancock. The boys were eager for action, but the veterans they met seemed content to be settling into winter quarters. The tired soldiers were just happy to be alive. They didn't talk much about their recent icy retreat from the Battle of Mine Run. Jem and Hank could see there wasn't going to be any excitement available until spring.

BY NEW YEAR'S DAY 1864, Hank had established a small business. He called it a business anyway. Some people weren't so sure.

"Who's got the fastest critter?" he would yell. That was the call for another roach race. The camp's mess hall was plagued with cockroaches, and at mealtimes soldiers would capture any that dared appear. Only medium-sized bugs were allowed in the races, none longer than an inch.

"First five that gets into the mug make up the race," Hank would announce.

The creatures of various shades and sizes were dropped into a regulation Army drinking cup held by one of the camp drummer boys. Bets were placed, and the roaches were then dumped into the small center ring of a big circle marked on the ground. Wild shouting built to crests of encouragement followed by troughs of woe as the race was not always to the swift. Often a slower bug made a direct run for the edge of the circle, while the most promising contestant wandered confusedly inside after all the others had crossed the line. Samson was frequently the big winner. Whenever there was a question about one of his cockroaches in a tie race, the matter was usually settled in Samson's favor. Since Hank was the organizer, he got a percentage from the total of the money bet on each race.

Of course, gambling was against regulations, but old Sergeant Evans pretended he didn't notice. He was a very different sort from Fatty Rat Snyder back at Camp Cass. Hard lines creased Evans's gaunt face, but they were not the marks of cruelty. He had fought in the Mexican War in 1847, and the Army was his whole life. The wise old sergeant knew that restless soldiers holed up in winter camp needed their little diversions.

Jem wasn't much interested in the racing. He got to wondering more and more what the Rebels were really like.

"Say, Hank," he asked one night when they met on picket duty at the edge of camp, "you think Johnny Reb is aching for glory as much as we are?"

"Hah!" puffed Hank, quickly spitting into the freezing darkness. "I guess he'd just have to be. He's bound to be pretty much like us. I wonder if he's getting as rich as I am racing lice. I hardly know what to do with it all. I'll be needing a barrel to keep it in before long, and then I'll need a wagon to haul it around. If money was glory, I'd have enough for both of us and we could head home right now, covered with it."

ON MARCH 23, GENERAL HANCOCK returned to his command of the Second Corps. He had spent the winter recuperating from a wound received the summer before at Gettysburg.

"Now, there's a soldier," said Hank. "Doesn't he look grand? No wonder they call him Hancock the Superb. I guess I'd like to be a general."

"Don't hang by your thumbs waiting," said Jem. The

six-foot officer, tall and straight on his horse, reminded him of the last time he had seen Pa. "He's been years getting to be a general."

"Give him some leeway," Hank retorted. "There wasn't a war to move him along. War speeds things up, you know. Our 'boy general' Barlow was a private just like us when he fought at First Bull Run. There's got to be hope for me."

Their admiration of General Hancock was soon forgotten. Feverish rumors flew from one regiment to the next about the expected arrival of an even grander figure, the new commander of all the armies of the United States. The man had already distinguished himself with hard-won victories in the west. President Lincoln had revived a special rank that no officer had held since George Washington. Lieutenant General Ulysses S. Grant just had to be the man to finish the war.

"I don't believe he's so glorious," said Hank in disgust the first time the dark-bearded, cigar-puffing hero of the battles of Vicksburg and Chattanooga rode into camp. "Look at that, will you? They say he can ride like the wind, but he sits on his horse like a sack of cornmeal."

Chapter Six

DAWN LIT THE PALE MIST drifting on the dark surface of the Rapidan River. The boots of the Second Corps made a dull, irregular thunder on the floating bridge at Ely's Ford. After all the drills at Camp Cass, Jem and Hank found it awkward to break stride. The engineers, who had worked hurriedly in the final hours of night, warned that the pontoon bridge would come apart under the steady pounding of marching in time. As they clumped along, Jem and Hank discussed the clover-shaped emblem on the square white battle flag fluttering in the gray light ahead of them. They wore the same emblem on their uniforms.

"I heard someone call it a trefoil," said Jem.

"Looks like the ace of clubs to me," retorted Hank.

"Ah, stop yer natterin'," said a voice behind them. "It's a shamrock, same as we have back in Ireland."

"Donovan," said Hank, "this side of the Atlantic we don't have any of your silly shamrocks, whatever they are, and I don't know what you're doing on this side of the ocean either."

"Sure, and on the other side there was neither food nor the money to buy it. Starve to death, it was, or leave the dear old country and cross the sea to Boston. I'd be there now if it weren't for the lively celebrations with friends the night before sailing, and being put on the wrong ship, and climbing off it in Baltimore. My uncle would have got me my job in the police, and my sweet Kathleen would be makin' our tea in the morning. For certain, I wouldn't be here educatin' the likes of yous."

"You might have avoided the likes of us if you had hopped a train to Boston," Hank remarked. "Then you could have done all your educating to the folks in Massachusetts."

"When I stepped off the boat, me boyo, I hadn't so much as a sixpence in my pocket. Not even a penny. And I was thinking I'll be starving to death same as if I'd stayed in Ireland. Then a fellow in an elegant coat and lovely top hat offers me three hundred dollars if I'll be so kind as to take his place in the Union Army. Take the money, I says to meself, and we'll be thinking about Boston a bit later."

"So here you are in our brigade," said Hank, "fixing to educate us, which is a notion that's much too uppity for a greenhorn."

"Well, now," said Donovan with a chuckle, "if an Irishman was to have such a thing as horns, wouldn't he be wanting them in green?"

"My ma says the Devil has horns, but I guess those would be red."

"You wouldn't be callin' me the Devil, now, would you?" said Donovan.

"No one was calling you anything," said Jem. "We were talking about the Second Corps trefoil."

"Ace of clubs."

"Shamrock."

"Quiet, men," snapped Sergeant Evans. "We're going into the woods now. Listen for the Rebs. It's them you'll be fighting today."

"It could be the ace of clubs," whispered Hank.

"Didn't you hear the sergeant?" hissed Samson Stiles. "You want to get shot? Your brains must be addled."

"Reveille at midnight and marching at two in the

morning's enough to addle anyone's brains," muttered Hank. "'Specially yours."

Samson's reply was lost in the crunching and cracking of dry branches as the Union troops forged through the tangled thickets. Dark pine trees spoiled the gentle promise of spring with their gloomy shadows, and gnarled oak trees threatened with a mysterious ancient menace. Local Virginians called these woods the Wilderness.

Each soldier wore a pack containing three days' rations, fifty rounds of ammunition, and a tent half that could be buttoned to another soldier's half to form a two-man tent. Jem found that sixty or seventy pounds tugging on his pack straps hour after hour became a painful burden for his shoulders. Furthermore, the unwieldy weight could throw him off balance if he tripped on a half-rotted tree trunk hidden in the dry leaves. As they crashed along, a heavy crackling thud was heard occasionally in the underbrush. It was always followed by loud curses. Hot language seemed to hover like splashes of bright color in the sultry air.

"My ma says you go to Hell for cussing," said Hank. "If she's right, there won't be room for standing come Judgment Day. Devil might run clean out of space to put all us sinners and be forced to rent some of the back forty acres in Heaven."

"The blabber you make," said Jem. "Rebs are bound to hear us, and then we could all get shot."

"I don't think so," replied Hank. "Johnny Reb's not here. His best chance was back when we crossed the Rapidan. And why hasn't he peppered at us while we're crashing and cussing through the woods? He's not here, that's why. No sir. No one's getting shot. Least not right now."

Samson crashed down like a dead tree in a storm. He lay among the brown leaves yelling the wildest oaths they had heard so far. Sergeant Evans dropped to his knees beside the writhing giant.

"Easy, Sam, easy. Just lay there a spell. Take it easy now. We'll carry you if you can't walk."

Samson groaned. "Put my foot in a fool woodchuck hole. Must have sprung my knee."

"That's all it is, is it?" Donovan sighed in relief. "And me thinking you was shot. Our first casualty we were having." A tight little ripple of nervous laughter went around the small group that had formed around Samson.

"It's no joke," said Evans. "The man's hurt. He's a casualty same as if Johnny Reb had put a bullet in that knee. We'll have to carry him to Chancellorsville. And you, Private Donovan, don't you be making light of casualties. We've had plenty before you joined up, and there's plenty more to come. You might even get to be one yourself."

Evans's reprimand cut off the fleeting moment of levity, and the heavy hand of tension gripped the company again. Everyone was silent.

As he lurched through the woods, Jem worried about being wounded. He had heard that a hospital was the most terrible place to be, maybe worse than death. Like everyone else in the brigade, he preferred not to speak his fear.

ON THE EVENING OF MAY 4, the Second Corps bivouacked in silence at Chancellorsville. Exactly one year before on the same ground, an unimaginably bloody battle had been fought. The Confederates were greatly outnumbered by the Union troops, but the Union's commander, General Joseph Hooker, dazed by a shell explosion, made a number of tactical blunders that resulted in a retreat for the Northern forces. When the smoke cleared, Union headquarters telegraphed President Lincoln that "Fighting Joe" Hooker had lost 17,000 Union soldiers. General Robert E. Lee had lost a quarter of his men, 13,000 soldiers, making it an extremely costly victory for the South.

"Didn't see hide nor hair of them," said Hank, pounding in a tent peg. "Rebs must have heard our cussing after all. Figured they better run 'cause close up it'd kill them deader than bullets. Just might at that."

Nobody laughed. No one even smiled. Older men, the veterans of last year, looked away into the woods. The growing darkness seemed ominous, more than simply the end of another day.

"Dawson," said Sergeant Evans quietly, "I don't believe you know what a fool you make of yourself with talk like that. The Confeds can fight just as hard as we can. We killed an awful lot of them here, but they killed more of us. I lost my best friend. Some of the men around you did the same. Look closer into them trees. See the white stripes? That's a rib cage washed clean by the winter rains. Could be my friend. See those other bones? They were all somebody's friend a year ago. Son, you better mind what you say."

Jem overheard the old sergeant's lecture and shivered. The campfire flickered in the gentle evening breeze. The shadows of the swaying trees gave an eerie life to the eyeless skulls leering from the woodland floor.

A gaunt, hollow-faced soldier Jem had never seen before was using a bayonet to scrape a shallow drainage trench around the neighboring tent. He levered a grimy yellowish skull out of the ground and rolled it toward Jem and Hank. It bumped to a halt, resting on the teeth of its upper jaw. The dark and empty eye sockets gaped straight at them, as though able to see a soldier's thoughts.

"That is what you are all coming to," said the sunken-cheeked soldier in a voice heavy with gloom. "And some of you will start toward it tomorrow."

Jem stared at the ghastly dome, his mind frozen by a grisly idea. Pa was here last year, he thought. That skull could have been a friend of his.

BY FIVE O'CLOCK IN THE morning, the Second Corps was marching. If they had gone a mere three and a half miles west along the Orange County Plank Road, they would have been in the right place. Instead, they marched briskly south and then west for six miles. At nine o'clock they were two miles beyond Todd's Tavern, in Spotsylvania County, when they received orders to go back.

"Well, shoot," said Hank, spitting into the dusty road, "why in tarnation didn't they tell us right off where we were supposed to stop?"

"Maybe they didn't know," said Jem.

"Didn't know what?" Hank asked. "Didn't know where to make a stand and fight the Rebs?"

"Maybe they don't know where the Rebs are."

"Seems like those Rebs spend all their time running. Must be they're the foxes and we're the hounds. Course the hounds generally win in the end. The fox just gets all tuckered out and can't run anymore."

"Hounds get tired, too," said Sergeant Evans. "Time this campaign's over, you'll know all about it."

They turned around and marched back along the dusty road. In the midday heat the return trip seemed to take twice as long. At Todd's Tavern they learned that they weren't through yet. Orders came from Grant's headquarters to march three miles north on Brock Road.

"It's just no use," grumbled Hank as he slung his Austrian rifle onto his shoulder, "no use at all to go camping and marching through half of creation if old Bobby Lee won't make his Rebs stand and fight."

Brock Road turned out to be no more than a track in the woods. There was no time to rest when they finally got to the Plank Road. Facing west on either side of the crossroads, they built entrenchments of earth and logs.

"Choppin' and diggin' and all," puffed Donovan. "I'd as soon be home cuttin' turf in the bogs."

"Puts me in mind of farm work," said Hank. "Just what we joined up to get away from."

"Well, it beats cleaning out the hen house," said Jem, although privately he had to admit there was something to what Hank said. The day so far had been nothing but a lot of heavy labor.

At four in the afternoon the Second Corps received yet another order from General Grant. This late in the day, they were to engage the enemy at last. Confederate General A. P. Hill was reported advancing his corps east on the Plank Road. General Hancock was instructed to attack and drive Hill's men back.

"Hoo-ee!" screeched Hank. "Here we come! Watch out, Johnny Reb. We're fixing to cut ourselves a piece of glory!"

"At last," sighed Jem, although he felt uncertain about finally facing action. The dry crackle of rifle fire rattled harshly back and forth for three hours, but no cannons boomed, since artillery was useless in the dense woods. Often Jem took aim at vague outlines he thought might be Confederate soldiers, only to watch the shapes melt into the thick underbrush. Sometimes he pulled the trigger anyway, feeling a strange relief that he had lost sight of his victim. This was different from their old game of Yank and Reb that Hank and he used to play coming home from school. Rifles weren't sticks. Once, while aiming at a Rebel, it crossed his mind that this was not like plugging rats around the corncrib at home with Pa's old twenty-two because, unlike the rats, the Confederates were firing back. Even though it seemed to be a matter of shoot or get shot, Jem had to wonder if he could ever get used to shooting real people.

When night fell, the exhausted troops dropped where they were, hoping for rest and silence. There was no silence. A general moaning drifted through the woods between the lines of battle. Lying against the base of an old oak, Jem couldn't tell where the sound was coming from. Sometimes it was louder, sometimes softer. It was the crying of the wounded, the sound of pain. Here and there a soldier pleaded for water. Occasionally, there was cursing when one of the thieves who followed the Army, waiting to pick the pockets of the dead after each battle, mistook a wounded soldier for a corpse.

"Crying of folks lost in Hell couldn't spook a fellow worse," whispered Hank.

For years afterward Jem's dreams would be haunted by the grim chorus of blood-soaked battlegrounds.

WOODLAND BIRDCALLS WOKE THEM AT dawn before the bugles sounded reveille. The scent of spring wildflowers drifted in the crystal air, mingling with the rich smell coming from the pots of coffee brewing over campfires. Coffee and rocklike biscuits called hardtack made a hasty breakfast before the lines of battle were formed again. In two hours of fierce combat Hancock's corps pushed Hill's weary men less than a mile west. Meanwhile, fresh Confederate troops filtered through the woods to reinforce Hill's men and turn the Second Corps back eastward toward their entrenchment on Brock Road.

"We're going the wrong way," gasped Hank as they jogged through the dry leaves and bracken.

"Johnny Reb's makin' it too hot to stay put," shouted Donovan.

"I think we're going the right way," yelled Jem, "at least for the time being. We can try again later."

"I'd rather be going the other way," said Hank.

"I'm thinkin' you'd be makin' the trip alone," replied Donovan. "But there'd be company soon enough, Federal company, while starvin' in one of them Rebel prison camps."

"You're wrong as usual, Donovan," said Jem, stopping suddenly. "We've got company already. Look yonder down the road. Blue jackets coming toward us."

In fact, there were clean blue uniforms all around them, and the road was jammed with horses and wagons. The reinforcements swept in among the retreating soldiers, and no one knew which way to go. There was so much confusion that General Hancock had no choice but to order everyone to fall back and strengthen the Brock Road breastworks.

"Jumping juniper," said Hank. "Here we are digging again. Should have turned around and gone west after all."

"You'd likely be diggin' for General Hill instead of General Hancock," said Donovan.

"I'd take the risk."

"Would you, now? Even with Johnny Reb holdin' a rifle to your spine?"

In midafternoon they dropped their shovels and jumped

into the trench. Confederate troops were moving up through the woods. Jem was startled to see real soldiers appearing crisp and clear in the dappled sunlight. Soon there was fierce fighting right in front of the breastworks. They really mean it, thought Jem when a small group of Rebels struggled to plant a square red battle flag with its white stars and blue bars in the freshly dug earth. One boy in gray fell at their feet in the bottom of the trench. Donovan was on top of him like a terrier and quickly ran a bayonet through the lad's throat.

Jem felt slightly queasy as he and Hank returned to the job of shooting at any Confederate soldiers they could see in the underbrush, but there was no time to be sick. Those fellows are aiming to kill me, he thought, and I've got to kill them first.

In spite of the wild shouting and screaming punctuating the constant racket of rifle fire, fighting was beginning to seem like a job almost as routine as chores on the farm. Even the air, becoming increasingly heavy with gunsmoke, seemed quite ordinary until Jem suddenly recognized the smell of a very different sort of smoke.

"Fire!" he yelled.

"That's what we're doing," shouted Hank.

"No!" retorted Jem. "Forest fire!"

The dry woods in front of them suddenly became a wall of flames. With the wind at their backs, a line of Rebels came whirling through the fire, yipping their high-pitched, spine-chilling Rebel yell. The Union troops climbed up and over their own earthworks, shouting their deeper-pitched battle cry to drive the Confederates back into the flaming woods. They were then driven back themselves.

As the boys returned to their positions in the trench, Jem and Hank saw a shadowy figure on horseback shrouded by smoke billowing from a flaming thicket. They both lifted their rifles to shoot as a momentary fluke in the wind shifted the low-lying smoke. Jem gasped and dropped his weapon. The man looked just like Granddad, even to the gray mustache. The horse, which had been frozen in panic, now wheeled suddenly and galloped into the blackened woods.

The heat became searing as the fire scorched over the earthworks. Choking on the smoke-filled air, Jem and Hank took shelter in the bottom of the trench. Up above they could hear screams of agony piercing the roaring storm as it shriveled up the trees. Confederate and Union wounded lay together, helpless in the flaming woods.

The fire died out along with the daylight. Exhausted troops crawled onto the earthworks and sat in the cool night air, stunned. Jem stared at some small flames still flickering on and off at the edge of the woods. The image of the gray-mustached Confederate officer was fixed in his brain.

"What if we had shot him?" he mumbled.

"Shot who?" asked Hank, scowling.

"Granddad."

"Granddad! Your granddad? Oh, you mean the Reb officer with the gray mustache. He was a Reb, wasn't he? Aren't we supposed to shoot Rebs? Would have shot him, too, but we didn't have time to draw a bead on him. And I don't believe for one minute he really was your granddad."

"Bound to be somebody's granddad," murmured Jem to the glowing embers.

Chapter Seven

THE TRANQUIL MAY MORNING AIR was blasted by a Union marching song. Every company in the brigade bellowed in unison. "Yes, we'll rally round the flag, boys, rally once again." Then the other brigades in Barlow's division picked it up. "Shout-ing the battle cry of free-dom!" Jem tried to imagine the whole of General Hancock's Second Corps singing. "We will rally from the hillside, we'll gather from the plain." Maybe the entire Army of the Potomac was one voice today. Could a hundred thousand roaring men wake up Confederate President Jefferson Davis, fifty miles away in Richmond? Of course not, thought Jem, but such a vocal crescendo would probably be more of a shock to the Confederacy than they'd been able to deliver so far. In the Virginia Wilderness, Lee's raggedy forces had been outnumbered almost two to one. Nevertheless, they had defeated Grant's enormous Army.

"What are we singing for?" asked Jem.

"We're happy," replied Hank, "aren't we?"

"And it's alive we are today," said Donovan.

"A lot of us aren't," said Jem. "I heard a couple of colonels talking. Said we had more than ten thousand casualties in the last two days."

"Well now, it's for our own selves we're dyin', isn't it? Jamie-boy, there's none can tell you how many Irish lads have died in English armies fighting for English kings."

"Some are saying we lost nearer twenty thousand."

"Cheer up," said Hank. "At least we're not retreating. We're still going south to Richmond. Didn't you hear old Evans when we were having our coffee? Four generals before Grant, and none of them had the guts to advance after a setback. That's worth singing about."

"Right you are," said Donovan. "But there's a small question I have. Where's that General Bob Lee got to, I wonder?"

LEE AND HIS ARMY OF Northern Virginia were waiting for the Army of the Potomac a way down the road at the little village of Spotsylvania. The Confederates had labored for two days to build strong entrenchments just north of Spotsylvania Court House. The middle section of these fortifications was a round arc, which projected almost a mile beyond the main line. On May 10 Union forces were turned back from their effort to break through this "Mule Shoe," as the soldiers had named it.

"Grant picked the wrong men for the job," said Hank.

"And it's more than pleased we'd be to help him out." Donovan chuckled. "We only need askin'."

"Boy Barlow's Boys," said Jem proudly.

General Francis C. Barlow was a slender, smooth-faced Harvard graduate who had been practicing law in New York City when the war broke out. He had joined the Army as a private, but because of his energy and enterprise he had been promoted rapidly up the ranks. A checkered flannel shirt was always visible under his unbuttoned officer's tunic, and on his left hip he slung a hefty cavalry saber. He brought a wild enthusiasm to the business of war, and the soldiers in his division were fiercely enthusiastic about their "boy general."

They needed every bit of that enthusiasm on the night of May 11. Barlow's Boys and two other divisions of Hancock's

60

Second Corps were ordered to march to the front curve of the Mule Shoe. A march in darkness over unknown ground was always hard. This one was made in the pouring rain.

"Too much," grumbled Hank. "Too much and not enough. Too much mud and not enough victory."

"Is it victory on a silver platter you're wanting?" asked Donovan. "You have to work for it, lad. And this here's no worse than a middlin' storm in the bogs. I've seen it much wetter."

"Our colonel thought this was bad enough," said Jem, taking the soggy cap off his head. "He was mad. Said the whole night's work was madness."

"We were standing there, too," said Donovan, "and you've told only half the story. Sure, and upon the word 'madness' the Boy General laughed out loud," said Donovan.

"Like to fell off his horse laughing," said Hank sourly.

"This march is for laughin' or cryin', it is. And for myself, I'd choose laughin'. The better for fun."

"You crazy Irishman," muttered Hank.

"We might all be crazy," said Jem.

The events that came next were insane, indeed. Hancock ordered the attack at half past four in the morning. In five minutes Barlow's division and one other went yelling through the rain and fog to storm the breastworks of the Mule Shoe fortifications. Their frenzy as they tore through the terrified Confederates was like a human tornado.

Donovan brandished his bloody bayonet in the drenching rain as though he were a demented demon in a dark and watery hell. Galloping like a wild horse, Hank screamed furiously, his eyes fit to pop from their sockets. Jem clutched the barrel of his rifle and swung it, cracking skulls with the butt. Sergeant Evans jogged steadily along, methodically ramming his bayonet into the gut of every Rebel who turned to face him. In the sheeting rain the battleground became a squelching swamp of mud and blood.

Then the Federals were driven back. Within the Mule Shoe the mad fighting raged back and forth for the rest of the day. Men fell. Large trees fell. The shooting did not stop until midnight. The light of dawn revealed enormous piles of soldiers, a few arms and legs still twitching, pinned under the weight of dead bodies.

AFTER A WEEK OF FURTHER fighting around Spotsylvania, Hancock made one more effort to break the Confederate line. Jem and Hank found themselves in the Mule Shoe again. The air was heavy with the stench of rotting corpses, and flesh had fallen from the faces of the dead.

"I wouldn't have believed it," gasped Hank, trying to block the stench by stuffing young spring willow leaves up his nose. "Pee-yew! I don't believe it now."

"Look . . ." gasped Jem. He threw up. He pointed at a corpse and then vomited again. "Look . . ."

It was Donovan's swollen corpse, covered with writhing maggots.

AS SPRING REACHED FOR SUMMER, Grant tried repeatedly to sweep eastward around Lee's Army and then move south behind it. When the Second Corps marched south on the Telegraph Road toward Richmond, they began to gain a peculiar sense of progress. At least the Army of the Potomac was now much closer to the Confederate capital than it was to the Union capital. By the time they reached the North Anna River, they had an almost invincible feeling that they were rolling like a human tidal wave that would swamp Richmond.

"When we get there," said Jem, "it'll all be over. Soon as we're dismissed, I want to head out and to see some more states besides just Maryland and Virginia. Could do it pretty easy with the railroads growing all over the country."

"Let's do it," replied Hank. "Let's go way out west. We'll get rich mining gold and silver in the Nevada Territory."

"Nevada's going to become a state any day now," mused Jem. "Probably it'll be one by the time we can get there. Before we head out, though, I'd like a little detour through Gaithersburg to find out about my pa and granddad."

"No-siree!" yelped Hank. "We can't do that! If we go back to Gaithersburg, we might never get out again."

"Counting your chickens too soon," Sergeant Evans said. "You boys weren't here before Grant. Can't tell you how many times, just when we thought we were getting someplace, it turned out we were stumped. Back when General McClellan was running this show, the Army wasn't winning any prizes for smart action. Confeds were always smarter and faster. Grant may be moving us in the right direction now, but hard as he's tried, he hasn't had much luck pepping up that old slow Army style."

"Who's to say, Sergeant," said Hank. "We're running through new country now. At least we're not fighting on ground that we've already fought on before."

"Like I said," replied Evans, "and I guess like you said, too, we're headed the right way, but beyond that, youngster, I don't care a hoot in Hell what you say. It don't mean anything until we're all in Richmond. I'm still waiting."

ON THE NIGHT OF JUNE 1, the Second Corps got lost in deep woods. An officer of topographical engineers had chosen a shortcut for the march to a lonely crossroads called Cold

Harbor. Although the road wound through swampy low country, it was layered with inches of dust that rose in clouds as the troops tramped along. Eventually, the way dwindled to a mere trail in the shadowed darkness, and the artillery units were unable to travel among the trees. They were forced to double back, causing the infantry units to reverse in total confusion. The so-called shortcut became a forced countermarch, resulting in twice the intended mileage, and the dust-coated men were badly fatigued and extremely hungry.

"I could eat a horse," coughed Hank.

"Horse meat's not half bad," said Sergeant Evans. "We might have to try some soon. That or forage."

"I guess horse couldn't be any worse than salt pork and beans, beans, beans," said Hank, "but I do favor foraging. Come daylight we might see some woods critters. How about a fat old possum, or even a couple of deer? I can almost taste a nice venison steak."

"Where are the supply wagons?" asked Jem as he fell again in the dismal darkness.

"Can't keep up with us," answered Evans.

"Grant's in too much of a hurry," said Hank.

"No," said Evans. "The wagons can't travel easy through this wet country. Even the roads and trails get swampy. Maybe they'll switch to pack mules."

"I guess I'd as soon eat mule as any other critter," Hank said.

COLD HARBOR WAS LIKE A small desert, quite the opposite of cold, and there was not even a puddle of water nearby that might have been called a harbor. Lee's cavalry and some infantry had already dug into the dusty hillocks and flats around the crossroads, where there had been some brisk skirmishing back and forth with a tough unit of Federal cavalry. Their commander, feisty General Philip Sheridan, was now sending messages that his raiders were in desperate need of infantry support. As the exhausted Second Corps was dragging itself into a ragged line of battle, an order came from Grant to attack immediately. The usually aggressive General Hancock insisted that his men needed time to rest up. The attack was postponed until dawn the next day.

"Looks like Johnny's been putting a whole lot of work into those fortifications," observed Jem as he crawled into the tent that evening.

"Does seem so," Hank replied, "but then he's got to be tired and hungry, too, just like Barlow's Boys here. Why, I bet those Rebs are beat right down to the sod."

"I suppose they would be at that."

"What in tarnation you doing?" said Hank, craning his head in the lantern light. "Scratching on paper? Jem-boy, I've never known you to write a letter home before."

"Not a letter. No one there could read it. Well, my granddad might if he ever got home again, but he's got to be so mad at me, I don't want him to know where I am. I'm just writing down my name and hometown to put inside my shirt so folks'll know who I was when I get shot."

The fragrant aroma of azaleas and swamp magnolias was floating in the still night air when General W. F. "Baldy" Smith's Eighteenth Corps moved in alongside. They had been transferred from the Army of the James River to double the strength of the Second Corps for the dawn attack.

AT FIRST LIGHT, BARLOW'S BOYS charged a sunken farm road, rousting out the Rebel sharpshooters who were using it as a trench, and then swooped on to overwhelm the Confederate line and capture three cannons. It looked like a major break-through until a deadly crossfire on either side of them caught the brigade in a pocket and prevented reinforcements from charging up to help, leaving Jem and Hank's brigade stranded. They were driven back a short distance by a fiery sheet of Confederate infantry bullets, but they could not retreat all the way.

"Jehosaphat!" said Hank, stretched as flat as a shadow on the ground and spitting dirt. "Can't stand up to run or we'll get shot. Can't even raise our heads enough to shoot back."

"Dig in, boys!" roared Sergeant Evans. "Use your fin-gernails if you have to."

Jem pulled the bayonet off his rifle barrel and started scraping the soil in front of his nose. Soon there was enough loose dirt under his chin for him to start scooping it with his tin drinking cup to make a minimal earthworks in front of his face. Every man in the brigade was doing the same thing, and in a surprisingly short time each one had scraped out a shallow depression that offered him some modest protection from enemy fire.

"With a little more work," grunted Hank, "we could dig our own graves."

Graves don't have to be six feet deep and cold, thought Jem. The one I'm in seems hardly six inches deep and hotter than Hell itself. At midday he drained the last drop in his canteen. Gradually, his tongue became coated with dust and his teeth began to squeak with grit. The permanent canopy of Rebel bullets whizzing low overhead made it impossible for him to go in search of more water, and crawling away to answer a call of nature would have cost him his life. Safety did not come until nightfall, when picks and shovels were brought up from the rear for feverishly digging deep trenches under the cover of darkness.

LATER THE NEW TRENCHES WERE reinforced with earthworks and logs. As days stretched into weeks and both sides dug in permanently, Jem realized that no one was going anywhere. He always dove for cover in the well-built trenches whenever the artillery batteries engaged in their frequent duels. No serious damage was done, however, and eventually the armies brought in special mortars, each weighing several tons, hefty vats that Jem thought resembled huge thick-sided pork barrels. Pointed at a much higher angle than the regular artillery cannons, these squat-looking guns could heave shells that would rise up into a tall arc and then drop like bombs down into trenches to kill or maim the occupants.

"It's downright spooky how they're tucked way back there," said Jem at noontime one day, "so far you can't see them and you don't even hear the shot until too late, when the shell is on its way down. Can't duck anyway. And if you try to climb out of the trench, you're nailed by a Reb minié ball."

"Yeah. But did you see them last night?" asked Hank. "Those fuses on the shells made a right pretty piece of fireworks in the sky."

"You can keep your show for the Fourth of July," Jem said scornfully. "The shells are scary. It's too easy to hit us. It's murder. Those guns should be outlawed. And we're doing it to them, too. It doesn't make sense and it doesn't seem fair."

Hank took a deep breath and sighed. "What's fair in war? And what isn't? We're all killing each other every which way. Who's to say what's fair? It's war."

Chapter Eight

AS THE VULTURES FLY, RICHMOND was only ten miles from Cold Harbor, and Lee's Army was even more battered and exhausted than Grant's.

"I bet we could take Richmond," boasted Hank. "Every time Grant has ordered a move, the Army pulls out to the left and then marches south, trying to slide in behind the Confeds. For once, why don't we pull out to the right and then head straight on down to Richmond? Shoot, if we moved real fast one night, we could be slamming clean through the city at dawn."

"That's plain crazy," said Jem, as he carved a piece of wood he was shaping into the hull of a model fishing sloop. "It would be like laying down at the lumber mill and putting your head in the buzz saw. Lee's sitting there like a big old cat, just waiting for us. His Rebs may be pretty tired, but they're pretty determined, too."

"Don't forget they're defending their capital," said Sergeant Evans. "Think how hard we'd fight if we were dug in around Washington with Old Abe sitting in the White House."

"Fighting, sure," replied Hank. "But what we've been doing these past weeks here doesn't seem much like fighting. I'd say something's got to change."

Change would be grand, Jem thought. We've sat for too long. One dark night on picket duty he had wondered if he should hightail it for home. Then he reminded himself that he would most likely be shot as a deserter. It would be down-right foolish to be killed by his own people when it was his idea to be here. No one had forced him or even politely invited him. I'm here, he thought, because I made the decision myself. I'll just have to stay put. But staying put in these stinking trenches is getting to be mighty boring. Yes, right about now I sure would like a change.

IN MID-JUNE THERE WAS A change so abrupt that even the soldiers' efficient grapevine didn't foreshadow it. The whole Army, except for Sheridan's cavalry, suddenly began to move, and it was not toward Richmond. Sheridan was supposed to keep Lee's troops distracted defending the Confederate capital while the rest of the Union Army started yet another wide swing east and south in an effort to get behind the Confederate Army. Grant's strategy lay in the hope that this time, diverted by Sheridan's activity, Lee might not realize that the Union troops were staging a major move. There was a serious risk that Lee would figure it out sooner rather than later, and if he could move his troops with their usual speed, it would be a colossal disaster for the Union. Grant was taking an enormous gamble.

"At least we're leaving those trenches," said Jem as the Second Corps began to march, "but I can't figure where we're going."

"If we could figure what's in Grant's head," said Sergeant Evans, "the enemy could figure out the plan, too. If it's a surprise for us, it's a surprise for General Lee."

ONCE AGAIN THE ARMY OUTRAN its supply lines and had to forage for food, but there were very few wild animals left in the woods. On a warm evening Sergeant Evans stood on the veranda of a tall brick farmhouse. A gaunt and hard-faced woman stared at him from the doorway she was barring with an ancient shotgun.

"The Dear Lord knows I can't stop you, Sergeant," she said, smoothing back a wisp of faded blond hair that had strayed across her haggard face. "I'm sure you'll take whatever you want. I just hope you can find it in your heart to leave us enough to keep body and soul together. But remember, Sergeant, no one steps into this house. I got my daughters to think of, and there's nothing in here of use to fighting men. This gun may look old, but it's loaded and it works. And I'm not afraid to use it. You hear?"

"Yes ma'am," said Evans. "I'll see my men behave like gentlemen."

"They lost that title the minute they set foot on the soil of Virginia. Not that Yankees would ever know anything about being gentlemen in the first place."

She stepped back to close the front door. Jem, standing at the foot of the veranda steps, glimpsed a blond girl in the lamplight of the hallway. She looked fifteen or so, a much younger version of the woman with the shotgun.

"Let's go, men," said Evans. "Corporal Harrison, take two men to the chicken coop. Round up as many hens as you can catch and meet us at the smokehouse. Leave the eggs for the family. Bridwell, Dawson, come with me to the barn. See what livestock is there. We'll hitch up a wagon, if there is one, to haul the meat from the smokehouse. Let's be quick. Can't stay here too long."

"What we're doing here is downright wrong," Jem muttered to Hank. They were standing inside the barn, hitching a mismatched and scrawny team of horses to a rickety wagon by the yellow light of two lanterns.

"Foraging?" Hank asked. "Come on, Jem-boy. It's part of the war."

"It's against general orders."

"You heard any general orders since we left winter quarters?"

"Seems like stealing to me."

"Sergeant asked permission, didn't he?"

"That doesn't make it not stealing," said Jem. "Besides, what could that woman say? She had no choice. Supposing she said no? You figure that would stop us?"

"Maybe you'd rather go hungry."

"I'd rather not steal."

"Shoot, Jem-boy. We're not doing this because we want to have a little fun. We're doing it because we have to. Got no choice with our supplies not coming through."

"I wish there was another way."

"We've shot every last deer, rabbit, possum, squirrel, and bird in the woods. Whatever the Rebs didn't get to first. Hunting's all played out unless you want to go after the rats in that corncrib yonder."

"Might be better than stealing."

"Jumping juniper! I believe you really would eat a rat. You want him roasted whole or served up in a stew?"

"Maybe just fried. Hank, you can't help but see it. We're taking food away from that family in the house."

"They're Confeds, aren't they? Isn't that who we're fighting?"

"We're not fighting women and children."

"No. But if we don't grab the grub, we'll just be leaving it for the Rebs," said Hank as he tightened one last strap on the harness. He reached for his rifle, which was leaning against a board wall. "I'd rather feed ourselves than feed the enemy."

It was useless to argue with Hank. He plain can't see it, thought Jem. There's a lot more kinds of hardship in war than just hiking around the countryside to shoot and get shot up. But he couldn't discuss it with Hank anymore, so he tilted his head back and gazed up into the shadows high above the pool of flickering lamplight.

Gradually, the magnificence of the barn began to push aside reflections on war. It was the largest barn Jem had ever set foot in, and it was very old. The massive hand-hewn timbers were dark with age. Each joint in the frame was fitted so snugly, he couldn't have slipped a blade of grass into a crack. These joints were all fastened with wooden pegs. Probably there wasn't a single nail in the muscular old frame. The sturdy rafters soared into the darkness of the vast cavernous space under the roof like the ribs of a huge inverted ship.

"Will you just look at that loft," whispered Jem as though he were in a church. "I guess it could hold every load of hay I ever saw in my whole life. I wish I was out in the field with a scythe right now."

"You must be getting soft in the pumpkin," replied Hank, turning to face him. "Look me in the eye, boy. I said look." Jem looked. "Can you stand there and talk like you love the memory of farm chores? Now, I'm gonna look up there and tell you what that view puts in my mind."

Hank looked up and said, "I recollect one time when I had to sit in a pile of hay thinking about Seneca Creek and yawning my jaw off its hinges while you fiddled with a little toy boat you—" Abruptly Hank swung his rifle into position and fired a shot over Jem's head. Jem was so stunned, he never noticed the choked cry from high in the loft. But a moment later he heard a heavy thud on the floor behind him.

He whirled around with his rifle at the ready. Not three feet from where he had been standing lay the crumpled body of a Confederate soldier, his face buried in a pile of hay.

"I'll roll him over, Jem," said Hank, kneeling beside the body. "Stand by me, and if he so much as blinks, blow his brains out."

"I thought you were blowing my brains out," Jem said loudly, his head still reverberating with the sound of the explosion. "Scared me to kingdom come."

Hank rolled the soldier onto his back, and a gentle-looking young face lolled into the lamplight with its eyes like two green marbles staring fixedly into the darkness of the loft. Gazing at the still-bleeding corpse, Jem felt conflicting waves of sympathy and anger toward the dead youth, a fellow about his own age, who had tried to kill him. Jem was still frozen in a stupor of confused emotions when Sergeant Evans appeared breathlessly from the cattle stalls, leading a slat-ribbed cow.

"What kind of tomfoolery . . . ?"

"Done for," said Hank, looking up at Evans. "Buzzard was drawing a bead on Jem here. Would have drilled our boy for sure if I didn't happen to cut my eyes up to the loft just then."

"Fast shooting," said Evans, climbing up on the seat of the wagon. "Let's get this wagon out of the barn, and then you fellers just slide back in and drop those lanterns into the loose hay there. I'll be loading up the meat and the men at the smokehouse. We'll be waiting for you. Run hell-for-leather over there when the fire takes hold."

"No!" shouted Jem over his shoulder as he walked the lead horse through the barn door. "You can't burn this barn."

"Those are my orders, Private Bridwell," Evans said sharply. "Don't contradict me."

"But there's no need!" Jem yelled.

"You may think that, son, but there's all kinds of need. I said before, we've got to move out fast. You know what the farmers say: For every rat you see in the corncrib, there's ten more you can't see. We've seen one Reb. Could be a dozen more up there. Couple dozen. Can't let them chase after us when we leave. This is war, and I'm not used to explaining my orders."

Jem stood gasping as Evans drove slowly away. Then he turned to stare at Hank.

"Jem-boy! You look like you've seen a ghost."

"I just can't do it, Hank."

"I guess it puts you in mind of your own barn."

"Worse if there's folks inside."

"Rebs, Jem-boy. By now you should've got used to killing them. But knowing you like I do, since we were little tadpoles, I s'pose I should've known you wouldn't see this like most folks would. Put your heart at rest, Jem-boy, and wait for me. It doesn't take but one to light a fire. I'll be right back. Old Evans will never know you didn't follow orders."

Jem was still rooted to the spot when Hank reappeared through the smoke billowing out of the door. They had hardly rejoined Evans and the others when the flames began to flicker at the loft window.

"Bridwell and Dawson, watch here," barked the Sergeant. "Shoot any Rebs coming out this side. Harrison, take your two around to the other side in case they come out that way."

As Jem watched the flames licking through the roof shingles, his eyes filled with tears. He heard three shots crack out from the far side of the barn. In a moment one more shot popped, but the sound was almost lost in the crackling roar of the growing inferno. Planks of burning siding began crashing to the ground, and the spectacle gradually transformed into a different shape, with waving fringes of flame outlining the majestic timber skeleton of the barn.

As he backed away from the increasing furnacelike heat, Jem became aware of a fluttering to his left. He looked over and saw a skirted figure ten feet away. It was the girl he had seen in the hallway. The breeze at her back was blowing her blond hair in front of her face. A lock of it dropped to her shoulder for a moment. By the light of the fire, Jem could see the winking gleam of tears streaming down her pretty face. He wanted to go over to comfort her and tell her he understood.

But he knew there was no understanding.

Chapter Nine

GRANT'S LUCK WAS HOLDING. After secretly leaving the Richmond area, his Army was traveling by several different routes toward Petersburg, twenty-five miles to the south. All the southern railroads that supplied the Confederate Army were routed through Petersburg. If those tracks could be cut, Richmond and Lee's troops would be isolated from the rest of the Confederacy. The war would end quickly.

After the barn-burning incident, Jem and Hank slogged through swamps with Barlow's Boys, crossed the Chickahominy River, marched south to the James River, and stopped near Charles City Court House.

"Business as usual," said Hank. "Hurry up and wait."

"Anybody know what we're waiting for?" asked Jem.

"Ferries," Sergeant Evans replied.

"Ferries!" erupted Hank. "Well, that just about beats everything. We're sitting here waiting for ferries, and out there they're building what looks to be the longest floating bridge in the world." He pointed to the middle of the river. Dark shadows rumbled and banged to the echoing direction of muffled voices where Army engineers were linking a hundred pontoons across more than two thousand feet of open water. At midstream the bridge had a swing section to let riverboats through, and for added stability the central assembly was tied to several schooners anchored upstream. "We couldn't just march over, home free with dry feet. No-siree. We got to do it the hard way."

"We're leading the Army," said Evans. "And it's better than swimming. We'll be across and outside Petersburg before the Ninth Corps or the Fifth or the Sixth get to set foot on that bridge."

"Missed one," said Hank. "You didn't mention the Eighteenth. Maybe they're flyin'?"

"Next best thing," said Evans. "See those transports out there on the river? That's them. While we were wallowing in the Chickahominy Swamp, they sailed down the York River and out into Chesapeake Bay. Now they're coming up the James. We'll all be in position together in the morning. Be like old times."

"Didn't I say it?" said Hank. "We just got to do it the hard way. And Baldy Smith's men get to float around in luxury, like they're the Navy or somebody."

"Never mind," Jem said quietly. "We're Barlow's Boys, and we don't need any fancy comforts to get where we're going."

"Wake up!" barked Evans. "Shake a leg, men. The boats are here. Orders are we got to hustle to get to Harrison's Creek by morning."

Two days later Sergeant Evans, veteran of the Mexican War, was killed when Barlow's division stormed the main Confederate line.

LIEUTENANT COLONEL HENRY PLEASANTS, COMMANDER of the Forty-eighth Pennsylvania Regiment of General Ambrose Burnside's Ninth Corps, started the work that led to the most horrendous event of the summer. This former mining engineer happened to overhear two of his enlisted men who had been coal miners in peacetime. They figured it would be easy to blow a huge hole in the Confederate fortifications if they could just dig a mineshaft under them. Most officers and engineers in the chain of command all the way up to Grant scoffed at the tunnel. They said that it would have to be much too long, the men would suffocate, and the Confederates were bound to discover it before it could be finished. Grant, however, was desperate for ideas that might break the siege, and Burnside wanted to keep his troops busy, so the plan was approved, and at the end of June the Pennsylvania soldiers began digging.

"And we're going to miss the fireworks," grumbled Hank. "Here we are, fooling around on a river again."

General Grant had ordered the Second Corps to cross the James River again and move back north to Richmond. The idea was to get Lee to detach troops from Petersburg and weaken the Confederate defenses. This would make it easier for the Union to break through when the mineshaft was blown up.

"We're on an important mission," said Jem. "That new sergeant said we're diverting some of Lee's troops. Who knows, Hank. Maybe this time we'll really take Richmond and the war will be over. Whew!"

"I say we're on a wild goose chase. They'll never get clean through without us there to show them how."

"Maybe it'll never happen," said Jem. "Lots of folks think the mine idea is plain crazy."

"But it just might work, Jem-boy. Those miners must know their business. And they're real tough."

"Tough's not worth much if you're all worn out. Think of it, Hank. The whole Army's getting frazzled. All spring we marched by night and fought by day. We got so tuckered out, we just sat in front of Petersburg and watched the Rebs."

"You could be right about that, Jem-boy. Word is even General Hancock is getting ornery."

"I know," Jem replied thoughtfully. "They say his old Gettysburg wound troubles him a lot."

As it turned out, Jem and Hank got back to Petersburg before the mine was blown up. The miners had been digging for a month. The entrance to the five-foot-high tunnel was behind the Union line. From there it ran more than five hundred feet to a wide chamber under a Confederate artillery battery commanded by Major William J. Pegram. Midway along the tunnel there was a ventilation duct, which was designed to draw fresh air to the miners working underground. The end of the duct that was aboveground was concealed from Rebel view by a clump of bushes.

"You should be happy," said Jem. "We made it back in time for the grand fireworks."

"Yeah," Hank replied, "but we just get to sit and watch. Heard tell a fellow called Brigadier General Ferraro has been training that Negro division in Burnside's corps to lead the way through the hole."

"I guess that's fair enough. A bunch of Burnside's men thought the whole thing up. They should get the satisfaction of finishing the job."

Three hundred twenty kegs of gunpowder were hauled into the tunnel. In the chamber under Pegram's artillery battery, the miners packed those eight thousand pounds of powder for the blast. At dawn on July 30, Colonel Pleasants lit the fuse.

Jem and Hank felt the earth tremble beneath their feet. A huge section of Confederate fortifications thundered up into the air on a column of orange and yellow fire flowered with billowing smoke. For almost a full minute the mass was the shape of a sheaf of harvested corn standing in a meadow. Then the towering image collapsed in a whirling deluge of men, cannons, horses, wagon wheels, and human body parts.

"Jee-hosaphat," whispered Hank. Jem didn't hear. He stared in stunned silence at the vast clouds of smoke and dust drifting lazily over the scene. In his experience of the horrors of war, he had never witnessed such a horrendous cataclysm.

The colossal explosion confused everyone so much that it was an hour before the Ninth Corps began to move. At the last minute Grant had told Burnside that the Negro division could not lead, because if anything went wrong, they would look like sacrificial lambs. They must be held in reserve to follow up if the attack was successful. Then, instead of running around the rim of the crater, other Union troops poured into it, but they had a terrible time trying to scale the opposite bank. Soon there were thousands of blue-clad soldiers in a giant human whirlpool. A good number of them managed to scramble up over the edge to fight their way beyond the crater, but they were finally driven back. The Confederates moved to the rim and started shooting into the crater. They brought up cannons and mortars to bombard the men at the bottom. By early afternoon the trapped Union troops began to surrender.

"Another disaster," cried Hank that evening. "It was like shooting fish in a barrel."

"I wish I hadn't seen it," said Jem tensely.

"Wouldn't have looked like that if *we'd* led the charge," said Hank bitterly. "Old Man Hancock wouldn't ever let a slaughter like that happen. He'd have had us around that hole and clean out the other side of Petersburg before Johnny could see through the smoke."

"I guess there'd be as many dead no matter how that fight went. Where's it getting us, Hank? There's been thousands killed, both Rebs and Yanks. Nobody's winning, and you and I could just as easy be the ones lying dead in the bottom of that hole."

The battle, fought under the blazing summer sun, had been short and brutal. It had lasted half a day. The Confederacy had lost fifteen hundred men, the Union well over four thousand. When darkness fell, the lines of the siege of Petersburg were drawn the same as they had been for weeks.

On a hot August afternoon, a couple of platoons of Barlow's Boys lay soaking in the Appomattox River about five miles upstream from the James estuary. As it was a Sunday with no fighting, there had been a lot of whooping and splashing. Freshly washed garments were spread on the riverbank to dry. Jem and Hank were lazing in the shallows.

"You're asking me for advice I can't give you," said Hank. "I don't even have a pa to worry about."

"Lately I been thinking about my pa a lot," replied Jem. "I had to tell you sooner or later. And besides, you knew him."

"Know him, Jem-boy, I know him. Not 'knew.' Don't talk like he's dead and gone before you learn it for sure."

"Remember camping at Chancellorsville before our first battle? Remember all those bones in the Wilderness? Lots of times I worry we'll get to be just another pile of bones. And I always worry Pa will, too. Maybe he's already nothing but bones."

"And that Reb officer with the gray mustache," said Hank, "the one in the forest fire? He got you all riled up about your granddad. I don't mean no offense, Jem-boy, but you're a regular old broody hen."

"I guess I'm more worried about Pa. I loved him and looked up to him as much as any boy could look up to his pa, but we were starting something kind of different last year. Seemed like we were just beginning to know each other as two men when he had to go back to war. I sure hope we have a chance to get on with that new kind of knowing."

"I believe you already know him better than you might figure," said Hank. "You know yourself, don't you? You and your pa are alike as two peas in a pod. Couple of years from now you'll be taken for brothers. The broody brothers."

"I always thought you and I were like brothers."

"Have to be, with what we've been through. And we grew up together. You had no ma and I had no pa. Neither one of us had real blood brothers. It just kind of falls into place. Don't look alike. Don't act alike. But we're brothers, Jem-boy, brothers forever."

There was a distant cry from across the water.

"Halloo . . . Billy . . . halloo . . . Billy . . . Yank."

Everyone sat up in a hurry. Some looked across the river. Others looked nervously at their clothes and rifles lying on the bank.

"Red fire and scorching brimstones!" said Hank. "It's a detachment of Rebs!"

A bunch of men and boys in faded butternut outfits were gathering on the far shore, but they didn't look much like a military detachment. Many of them were peeling off their tattered clothes as fast as the Union soldiers had shucked their blues an hour before.

Hank stood up in the water and called back, his hands cupped on either side of his mouth.

"HALLOO . . . YOURSELF . . . JOHNNY REB. . . . REAL . . . FINE . . . SWIMMING . . . TODAY."

"Hank! You crazy coot!" sputtered Jem. "What if they start shooting? And us with our rifles up on the bank."

"If they meant to, they'd have done it already, but it's a tad far even for a real good sharpshooter," said Hank. "Think they'll waste ammunition at that distance? Just to scare a few Yankee boys out of the water? Besides, it's Sunday. And also besides, I got another money maker in mind." He turned to the river again.

"GOT . . . ANY . . . TOBACCO?"

"Loads . . . Billy."

"WANT . . . TO . . . TRADE . . . SOME?"

"What . . . ya . . . offerin'?"

"YOU . . . LIKE . . . COFFEE?"

"Can't . . . remember.   Been . . . clean . . . out . . . for . . . weeks."

"COFFEE . . . FOR . . . TOBACCO. . . . OUNCE . . . FOR . . . OUNCE."

"River's . . . deep. You . . . got . . . flying . . . coffee . . . beans?"

"WAIT . . . JOHNNY. . . . YOU'LL . . . SEE."

"Don't . . . know . . . any . . . flying . . . tobacco . . . neither."

"JUST . . . YOU . . . WATCH . . . REB."

Hank turned to Zeke, the new bugle boy. "Run up to camp and bring back a pound of coffee." Then he looked at Jem. "Where's that little boat you been working on?"

"Just up the bank," said Jem. "I figured to finish the last bits of rigging and try her out after we finished swimming."

"Think she'll haul a cargo?"

"She might hold a right small one."

"Could we sail her over to Johnny Reb?"

"I don't know, Hank. It's just a light breeze coming up the river. I guess she could make it on a broad reach, and if you're thinking what I'm thinking, Johnny could just swing the sails over and send her back. But you better be sure he does. She's the best I've done, and I was thinking about giving her to my granddad if I ever see him again—although, come to think of it, I don't know how I could carry her in my pack all the way home to Maryland without crushing the spars and rigging."

The bugle boy came back, breathing hard and carrying his cap filled with coffee beans. Jem was already making minor adjustments in the rigging of the *Star of Maryland* as she floated in the shallows. Hank folded two small paper packets to hold the coffee, and Jem placed them on the deck, fore and aft. He set the boat loose on the water, and a cheer went up from the other shore.

"You . . . Yankees . . . might . . . be . . . right . . . smart . . . folks . . . after . . . all."

First the little craft balanced current against wind to sail straight across. Halfway over, she hit the main current and started sliding downriver. A couple of Rebels ran down the shore to where they guessed she might land. Then a gust of wind caught her, and she just about spilled the beans into the Appomattox, but she leveled off and sailed on, straight to shore. Jem heaved a deep sigh as he watched the Rebs turn the *Star of Maryland* around, loaded with tobacco.

"Here . . . she . . . comes . . . Billy. . . . Virginia's . . . best . . . tobacco."

"THANKS . . . JOHNNY."

"Fair . . . trade. . . . Say . . . Billy . . . got . . . any . . . sugar?"

But Hank didn't hear. He was already up on the bank, auctioning off the tiny cargo of tobacco, even before the little ship sailed into port.

Chapter Ten

_c✐_

EVER SINCE THE DISASTROUS MINE explosion and the slaughter that had followed it, the siege of Petersburg had settled into a boring and mostly stationary business for both Union and Confederate troops. A lot of energy on both sides was devoted to repairing, improving, and expanding fortifications. Wooden forts were mended where they had been damaged by snipers or shellfire. Trenches were dug deeper and lined with retaining walls made of tall earth-filled baskets woven out of bushes and small tree branches. Earthworks were reinforced, their fronts bristling with abatises made of sharpened saplings pointed outward so that charging enemy soldiers might be impaled.

In the Second Corps, a part of each day was taken up with drilling, marching, and spiffing up uniforms. Jem and Hank felt almost as though they were back in training camp, except they knew that if they showed their heads at any fortifications, they risked a Rebel sniper bullet in the face. At night things were a little more relaxed. Rebel fuel parties were allowed to gather firewood undisturbed. Union and Confederate pickets posted between the opposing lines came to know one another by name.

ONE MOONLESS AND MISTY NIGHT, Jem was on picket duty. The darkness dripped with gloom, and he felt as though there might be dangers other than Rebels hidden in the shadows—maybe ghosts of dead soldiers, or perhaps weird spirits much older than humans. Out of the corner of his left eye Jem saw a drifting rag of gray mist twitch suddenly. He gasped and swung his rifle to the ready, pointing the bayonet in the general area where he thought he had seen the motion. He wasn't sure if it was actually a person, so he felt silly trying to utter the standard "Who goes there?" He tried anyway and choked, coughing loudly.

"Easy does it, Anson," said a hoarse voice. "It's only me. Burnley. You don't want to shoot your best friend now, do ye?"

"Name's not Anson," snapped Jem.

"You foolin' me? You sure sound like him. Sounded like Anson coughing, too. Come on, now, you don't want to go pullin' stunts on a spooky night like this here."

"I'm not Anson," Jem repeated to the faceless darkness, "and I'm not fooling. Who are you?"

"I done told you, it's Burnley. And now you know my name, you might kindly tell me yourn."

"Jem."

"Well, Mr. Jem, I hope you ain't fixin' to shoot."

"Can't shoot what I can't see."

"That's real good, 'cause I think that's your bayonet pointin' right at my gullet." A ghostly hand reached out of the murky fog and gently pushed Jem's rifle barrel to one side. "You sound kinda Southern, so I thought you're Confederate for sure, but I'm beginnin' to wonder. Where you from?"

"Maryland," said Jem. "Where you from, Mr. Burnley?"

"Virginia. Up in the mountains, a little whipstitch called Fulks Run. Right pleased to meetcha." A pale gaunt face with a scraggly dark beard loomed dimly in the fog. The Reb dropped his hand from Jem's rifle and extended it for a handshake. In nervous astonishment Jem placed his rifle butt on the ground and slowly extended his own hand. They shook hands briefly and then stared at each other for a full minute in taut silence.

"Fulks Run," mused Jem. "We've got a Fulks family back home in Gaithersburg. They have a general store and a lumber business."

"Never heard of 'em," replied the Reb. "And I'm a Fulks myself. Burnley Fulks, but our people crossed over the Shenandoah River from Flint Hill, Virginia. We don't run no store neither. Just scratch away at a little dirt farm on the shoulder of a mountain."

"We have a farm, too," said Jem. "But I don't know if anybody's running it now. Field hands all ran off while my granddad was away."

"Field hands!" exclaimed Burnley. "Now don't that just beat all. You're in the Union Army and your folks own slaves. Me? I'm in the Confederate Army and my folks never owned slaves. Not even one."

"What is it you're fighting for?" asked Jem.

"Not for slaves. Couldn't afford none anyway. No-siree," said Burnley stoutly. "I don't hold with slavery, but I'm fighting for my country."

"Your country!" It was Jem's turn to exclaim. "That's what I'm fighting for."

"Not mine, you ain't," said Burnley. "My country's Virginia, and you Yankees are in it, breakin' up housekeepin' and makin' a general mess like a passel o' razorback hogs runnin' wild in the woods."

"Well, I don't hold with slavery either"—Jem sighed—"but my granddad does, and less than a year ago a raggedy troop of your boys tore up his place and burned the barn."

"Foraging, most likely," Burnley said quietly. "I remember

we had to do some of that around Sharpsburg. Ain't that your neck o' the woods?"

"Forty miles. We heard Antietam Creek was running blood. Seems like we just go on killing each other and making the earth swampy with blood. If it's ever over and done, will there be anything left for the survivors?"

"Will there be any survivors?"

The Yank and the Reb stood in silence for a while, and presently, from the direction of Petersburg, strains of a fiddle accompanying the voices of many men singing drifted through the fog:

> "Now here's to brave Virginia, the Old
>   Dominion State,
>   Who with the young Confederacy at last
>   has sealed her fate;
>   And spurred by her example, now other
>   states prepare
>   To hoist on high the Bonnie Blue Flag that
>   bears a single star."

"That's my boys," said Burnley. "We sing like that lots of nights."

"It's good strong music," Jem whispered as the chorus began:

> "Hurrah! Hurrah! for Southern rights,
>   hurrah!
>   Hurrah for the Bonnie Blue Flag that bears
>   a single star."

As the sound floated away on the night air, new voices emerged from the other side:

"The Union forever, hurrah, boys, hurrah!
Down with the traitor, up with the star;
While we rally round the flag, boys, rally
    once again,
Shouting the battle cry of freedom!

We are springing to the call for Three
    Hundred Thousand more,
Shouting the battle cry of freedom,
And we'll fill the vacant ranks of our
    brothers gone before,
Shouting the battle cry of freedom."

"That's right pretty," murmured Burnley.

"You call that pretty?" queried Jem. "That's our marching song. For pretty you should have heard them earlier, singing 'Lorena.'"

"Oh, I know that one," said the Reb, and very softly he sang,

". . . 'Twas flowery May,
When up the hilly slope we climbed,
To watch the dying of the day,
And hear the distant church bells chime.

We loved each other then, Lorena,
More than we ever dared to tell;
And what we might have been, Lorena,
Had but our lovings prospered well.

"Our boys sing 'Lorena' too."

IN THE LATE SUMMER AND into the fall, the Second Corps was ordered to harass the Rebels into extending their south-side fortifications farther and farther west in order to stretch Lee's exhausted and outnumbered troops as thin as possible. Rather than an organized offensive, the strategy was to worry the Confederates by digging new trenches ever westward and occasionally charging the trenches that the Rebels would build in response.

ONE CRISP NOVEMBER EVENING, AS the company charged once again across a bloody cornfield, Jem stared into an orange sunset, wheezing. He felt as if he must have died a dozen times that day. Now he would have to do it one more time, encrusted with sweat, dirt, and dried blood.

"If there were any Rebs out here," Hank panted, "you wouldn't be able to tell who was Johnny and who was Billy. We all look like we're made out of moving stone."

"I feel like stone," puffed Jem. "And some of us aren't moving anymore."

Just as he spoke, he fell over a corpse. Somebody's muddy boot squashed his left hand into the soft, blood-soaked earth. He struggled to get up. Running soldiers kept bumping into him, and one knocked him down again. Finally, he stood up, amidst the yelling and the thunder of cannons.

Jem staggered into a shambling run. He had to keep moving or he would be knocked down again. He strained for breath and clutched his rifle close to his belt. My last charge, he thought. I'm gonna die in this one. Won't have to charge ever again. Finally, they were stumbling up the slope of the Rebel earthworks. On the crest, in hand-to-hand combat, dark figures performed a dance of death like hellish black puppets set against the fiery western sky. Jem stopped to look around for Hank.

A weight, like a flying brick, grabbed his left leg, spinning him half around. As he fell on the breastworks, Jem screamed, but not because it hurt. Not yet. He screamed because he knew a Rebel bullet had torn a hole in his left thigh. He was going to lose the leg and maybe his life. Jem was mad.

In the midst of the tumult, a tall silhouette sprang from the Confederate trench. Looming against the sunset, it lurched clumsily over the earthworks, coming straight for him. With the last of his strength, Jem heaved himself up on his elbows, raised his rifle, and shot the dark soldier in the stomach. As the swaying figure twisted and toppled, the final red rays of the sun fell across a familiar face.

"I was coming back to find you," gasped Hank.

Chapter Eleven

❧

FIRST JEM THOUGHT HE HAD fallen in the icehouse back on the farm. Then he dreamed he was a corpse floating in the Appomattox River. It was time to get out of the river and dry off, but he couldn't. He wasn't in the river. He was already stretched out on the bank. Never had he felt so wet and cold and stiff. He opened his eyes and slowly rolled his head toward the river. There was no water. The embankment was Rebel defense works washed by the chilly light of dawn. The cold wetness was old sweat . . . and mud and blood.

Jem struggled to sit up. A hot orange wave of pain swept through him, and he fell back again. Darkness rolled over his thoughts. He slept.

THE SUN WAS HIGHER AND warmer when his eyes opened again. The cornfield was strangely quiet except for the cawing of a few crows. There should be moaning, thought Jem. The ambulance corps must have taken away the live ones. But why hadn't they carried him away, too?

"They gone on by this one."

"'Deed they gone on by," said a voice Jem knew well.

"Solomon," he croaked.

"I believe the boy knows you," said the first voice.

"Must have fever on the brain," said the second. "I never heard that voice before."

"Sounds like the old turkey buzzard pickin' at that body yonder."

Jem reached up toward the two figures standing against the bright morning sun. One of them bent down.

"Mist' Little-James? Oh, Lordy, Mist' Little-James, you's a mess, worse than a mess. You look like you's fixing to die. We gonta stop that, Mist' Little-James. 'Deed we will. Can't bury you in no grave. It's not your time."

"Solomon," Jem whispered.

"Yes, child. Gonta be all right," he said, kneeling.

"Water," Jem gasped.

"'Deed you need more than water, Mist' Little-James. We got to get you to the field hospital if it ain't packed up and moved on."

He trickled some water from a canteen into Jem's parched mouth and then started wiping his face with a wet cloth. It felt as good as a cool swim on a hot day. Solomon's strong gentle hands tried to straighten out the blood-soaked leg. Jem screeched. It was pain, pain, PAIN! He was wrapped in pain.

"Easy, Mist' Little-James, easy. You're hurting bad. Oh, Lord, you're gonta hurt more while we put you on this stretcher. But you're the first live body we've toted."

As the two men carried Jem along, he wondered how they had happened to find him. Talking to Solomon almost took his mind off the pain.

"What are you doing here, Solomon?"

"Well, Mist' Little-James, mostly we're burying folks."

"But didn't you go to join the Army?"

"I'm in the Army, Mist' Little-James, same as you. Only my job is different. Some of us get to be gun-toting fighting men, and some get to do other work. Some lays railroad tracks, and some buries the dead. Least we get paid. Never did work for money before. Plenty of work to a war. Plenty of money."

"But Solomon, Bertie said you wanted to help fight for freedom like a real soldier."

"I am a real soldier, Mist' James. Private Solomon Corn. I was in General Burnside's colored troops that didn't get sent into the crater. Was you at the Battle of the Crater, Mist' James?"

"I saw it, Solomon. It wasn't a battle. Just a terrible slaughter."

"Our Gen'l Ferraro trained us special to lead that attack. I was right sad when Gen'l Burnside said we wasn't gonta do it after all. But when I saw those poor boys dying in the crater, I said sombody's lookin' out for Solomon. Killing folks or burying them, I'm still a soldier. I'm a free man, Mist' James, just like you."

IN THE FIELD HOSPITAL UNDER a huge tent, the moaning and screaming was the worst Jem had ever heard. It was as though all the crying on all the battlefields of the war had been rolled into one awful symphony.

"Don't leave me here, Solomon."

"Can't leave you anywhere else, Mist' James. Someone might get to shoveling dirt on your face."

"Solomon! Solomon, stay with me. Please! Stay with me. I'll see you get extra pay when we go back to the farm after the war."

"Can't stay long, Mist' James. Just till we get you to the doctor. There's work yonder in the field. Can't come back to the farm neither. Never. You're going to live now, Mist' James. You tell Bertie you saw old Solomon. She'll be glad to know. And she'll know why I can't ever come back. I can't 'cause I'm a free man. I wasn't free on the farm, and I wouldn't feel free if I was to go back. 'Deed I wouldn't."

The smell of stale vomit and death floated heavily in the air. The basic stench was punctuated by wandering whiffs of anesthetics, sometimes the pungent odor of chloroform, sometimes the fermented aroma of whiskey. Although the general stink was sickening, it didn't take Jem's mind off the pain.

Solomon and his work partner sat on the ground beside Jem. Now and then they gave him a sip from his canteen. He noticed it was missing its shoulder strap, but he was hurting too much to wonder why. Solomon tried, in vain, to clean the wound. Every time he touched it, Jem howled like a monster from Hell.

"You's lucky, Mist' James."

"Lucky? You call getting shot lucky? The doctors are bound to saw this useless leg off. Then I might die anyway. Lucky?"

"You's lucky," Solomon repeated. "You's very lucky. Somebody done tied a strap around your leg to cut the bleeding. By yourself you'd have drained out all your blood on that field last night. We'd be laying you in a grave now instead of waiting on a doctor to fix you up. You just keep your mind on living. Somebody wanted for you to live."

Jem remembered the canteen strap. He had a dim memory of Hank cutting it off to use for a tourniquet. Lordy, where was Hank?

"Did you see Hank?" he cried, almost forgetting the pain for the moment. "You've got to find him and bring him back here. He's hurt real bad."

"Didn't see any Hank," murmured Solomon, "and how we gonta find him?"

"He's my messmate, my best friend. He's like a brother. You got to find him!"

"Now, how we gonta do that, Mist' James? How we gonta find that boy, with so many other folks laying out there?"

"You know what he looks like. He was with me on the breastworks. He's shot, too. You got to get him. You remember him, Solomon."

"'Deed I remember. I can't forget the two of you messing around in my barn. But it ain't no use, Mist' James. Was nobody laying by you when we found you. I expect Mist' Henry's in the cold ground now. But you's lucky. He must be the one tied the strap onto your leg."

Jem stared up at the dirty canvas overhead. Hank dead? he thought. And buried? The memory flickered again in his mind, clearer now. He could see Hank holding the canteen awkwardly. He was trying to cut the strap with a bowie knife. Jem wanted to talk to him, but no sound would come. He wanted to say that he stopped to turn back and look for Hank in the cornfield where he thought he had fallen. As Jem's mind slid into darkness again, he wondered, Have I killed him? Killed my best friend? Killed my brother? Solomon told me to keep my mind on living. How am I going to do that? I don't deserve to live.

THE FIELD SURGEON BENDING OVER Jem was more tired than anyone else in the hospital. The dark smudges under his eyes made him look haunted. Jem guessed he would be tired, too, if he had the doctor's job. He wouldn't want to see one body after another stretched out on this bloody table, waiting in pain to have an arm or a leg sawed off.

Brass buttons gleamed through the swamp of blood that soaked the surgeon's tunic front. Blood was all over the big tent, too. It seemed to drip from the screams and stench that filled the air. Then Jem noticed some activity just behind the doctor. Two men were piling human arms onto a blood-soaked stretcher. Behind them was a stack of legs, neat as a cord of firewood. A few of them still wore boots and socks. Some were oozing blood.

"Don't cut my leg off!" Jem screamed. "I'd rather die! No! I should die! Oh, Lordy Lord, you'd do better to cut off my head."

Three grim-looking orderlies were holding him down. They glanced at one another and took a tighter grip.

"Son," said the doctor, "that's a mighty bad wound you've got there, but you're lucky you—"

"Don't keep telling me I'm lucky! I'd be better off in my grave."

"Now, hold on, son! I'm trying to tell you something you need to hear. So shut up and listen. That's a flesh wound you've got there," said the doctor quietly. "It's deep, real deep. Must have damaged some muscle, but the bullet missed your thigh bone. It's not shattered. Do you hear me? That ball came close, but it did miss the bone. Now we have to dig it out of there. You just might keep that leg, son. It'll be a long time healing and it'll never be as good as the other one. Probably you'll limp a little. Might even need a cane. But you've got a chance to keep that leg. Now, there's plenty more wounded waiting for me, so let's get down to business. Sorry we're fresh out of chloroform. Have to use whiskey."

One of the orderlies was holding a bottle. With one hand he hauled hard on Jem's lower jaw to hold his mouth open. With the other he poured in a stream of scorching corn liquor. Jem thought he might choke to death. He coughed, and the orderly poured in another slug. A smelly rag was yanked tight between Jem's jaws. All three orderlies held him tight enough to break his bones.

"Pass me the bullet probe," said the surgeon.

Jem struggled to fight back. He tried kicking with his good leg, but the pain and a strange heaviness weighed him down. Once more he blacked out.

Chapter Twelve

❧

A BRASS BELL CLANGED IN the darkness, piercing the gurgling sound of rushing water. Strained creaks and wooden groans accompanied the slow tilting and heaving of the floor. Jem opened his eyes to the dim light of a swaying lantern and threw up. Vomiting and moaning echoed beyond where the shadows shrouded a sea of slow-moving bodies. The one beside him lay very still.

"Say, Hank." Jem coughed. "Where are we?"

"Name's not Hank," said the body, rolling over and vomiting beside Jem's stretcher. "But since you asked, we're on the cargo schooner *Amanda Bailey*."

"We're on a sailboat?"

"Should have been traveling in luxury on the steamer *Argo,* but she was still busy unloading medical supplies at City Point. The hospital wharf was getting crowded up with us wounded, and the *Bailey* was ready to leave for Washington. So here we are, puking our guts out."

Jem gasped and stared rigidly up into the swinging shadows. How could he have forgotten he had shot Hank? He'd never see him again. How was he going to live with that? He felt hot tears welling up. They trickled over his temples and puddled in his ears.

"If it hurts that bad," the man beside him said, coughing, "ask that orderly feller to get you some more morphine next time he comes through."

"No morphine can ever stop the pain inside," Jem whispered hoarsely. "It's going to stay inside of me until I die."

He could stand the grinding ache in his head and even the pain now flaming in his leg. It was the searing hole in his soul that was unbearable. Jem rolled off the stretcher onto the slippery floor. He buried his face in a bunch of vomit-soaked straw and pounded the boards with his fists.

The schooner kept on sailing through the choppy waters of Chesapeake Bay. As she approached the mouth of the Potomac, Jem heard a brisk voice shouting commands, while ropes and feet thumped on the deck overhead. The floor creaked slowly over to a new angle, and the bodies around him stirred and retched.

Never in his life had Jem felt so sick, so lonely, or so deep-down mad.

WASHINGTON WASN'T THE SLEEPY TOWN Jem vaguely remembered visiting with Pa ten years earlier. Here market day, race day, and a religious revival meeting seemed rolled into one grand hullabaloo. There were soldiers everywhere scattered among the traffic jams of horses, mules, and wagons, with lots of angry shouting at every crossroads.

A mule-drawn farm wagon had been requisitioned as their ambulance. It spent as much time stuck in traffic or mud as it did bumping and lurching through the smelly streets. Jem thought the pain would kill him for sure. Once they got so mired, it seemed as though they would have to get out of the wagon and push it. At last they moved.

"I don't rightly know if it's that ugly mule driver's cussing or the mules' ornery cussedness that got us going again," said Jem through teeth clenched in pain.

"Maybe both," said his grizzled companion from the schooner, who had finally given his name as Joshua.

"Most mules I know would rather stop than go," said Jem, "but not these critters. They surely don't want to stop."

"Not here, anyway," muttered Joshua.

Despite the confusion and noise and unsanitary stink, there was an odd spirit of exhilaration in the streets. Army supply wagons blocked each other at the intersections, their drivers yelling and then fighting. There were troops of soldiers marching every which way, some healthy, some not, some headed for the front, some coming back. A raggedy bunch of walking wounded straggled out behind the ambulance wagon, and some sickly-looking prisoners were being herded behind them.

"Whole lot of Union troops in town," Jem remarked, trying to distract himself from the pain in his leg. "A fellow might wonder if there's enough of them over in Virginia to fight the war."

"Yep," said his companion, "and Richmond's only a hundred miles away."

A half-built city was rising despite the war. In the distance Jem saw the nearly finished Capitol dome, resembling a giant sugar-fluted Easter egg nested upright on an oversized wedding cake. Even that past July, when Confederate General Jubal Early's troops had almost captured the city, foraging their way down the Frederick Pike through Gaithersburg and Rockville, the builders had kept on working. A good way off to the right was the unfinished base of what was to become the Washington Monument. There were stone blocks stacked up beside it, and beef cattle grazed in the surrounding meadows. The ambulance hauled up in front of a huge building. Jem thought it looked like a palace built for a king. It seemed pretty fancy for a hospital.

"Driver, I believe you made a mistake," said a pale, one-armed lad who looked quite a bit younger than Jem. "We may be worth our weight in gold, but you can't stash human flesh in a bank."

"Ain't no bank, whippersnapper," the mule driver said gruffly.

"Looks like the granddaddy bank of them all."

"This here's the United States Patent Office," explained the driver proudly. "And if you fellows hadn't gone and got yourselves all shot up, it would still be in business. Right now it's a temporary hospital, and a good one, too. Be glad I didn't get orders to take you to the one they slapped up overnight out on the Corcoran place. This here's better'n you deserve for your rest cure."

The mule driver scowled at the black stretcher bearers who had begun to gather around the wagon.

"Step lively, boys. Get these lazy heroes off my wagon. I got other calls to make."

WHEN ALL THE WOUNDED HAD been carried inside, a civilian doctor named Ludlow came around to study the damage. He looked at Jem's leg and shook his head.

"Those poor field surgeons get too many patients. Have to work fast and rough just to keep up. You know, you might have lost this leg."

"I thought sure I would, sir."

"Still could, young man. I have to tell you that. Your overworked doctor was forced to rearrange a lot of things to get the bullet out quickly. There seems to be a touch of infection here. I can see what we doctors call laudable pus, and if that's all you have, count yourself lucky. It could be a sign your leg is actually starting to heal. Any change—a whiff of gangrene, say—and we'll almost certainly have to amputate. For the time being, I'd say you're a lucky lad. Now, here's what . . ."

Jem stopped listening. Here was another person pronouncing him lucky. The doctor couldn't know about the awful pain deep inside, the burning anger. This Jem would carry to his dying day. He thought here, in this giant mausoleum, that day might turn up very soon. He even sort of hoped it would.

THE COTS OF THE WOUNDED were lined up among tall display cases with glass fronts. The shelves held models of contraptions people had dreamed up to be patented. There were various apple corers, different kinds of mousetraps, an underwater boat, even a flying machine you could get strapped into. If Jem had seen a horseless carriage among that collection of amazing inventions, it would not have surprised him.

At night the hall seemed truly haunted. There were only a few wisps of light from kerosene lanterns hung here and there. Ordinary noises became more spooky at night. The coughing of pneumonia patients echoed in the darkness. Soft, forlorn cries came from some who were actually hurting and others who were only dreaming. Once in a while a tormented howl would echo around the corridors. Jem figured it might be a sleeper who had turned over on his wound. Or it could be a soldier, wide awake, who couldn't stand the thought that he was missing an arm or a leg or a friend. Or a brother.

The sounds were made worse by the echoes, and the echoes were made worse by the darkness of night. Lying awake and listening was bad enough, but the dreams were worse. Sometimes he dreamed of jumping into Seneca

Creek. When he surfaced, he couldn't stay afloat and sank underwater again. He couldn't swim with only one leg.

"Hank!" he gurgled. "Pull me out! I'm drowning!"

Hank never answered, and Jem awoke in a sweat. He heard whispering all around him.

"Can't you get through one night without yelling?" hissed the Massachusetts lad next to him.

"Easy, boy," came the hoarse voice of an Illinois man on the other side. "It'll be better come dawn. Just lie still and watch for the first light."

Once Jem dreamed about explaining to Pa.

"I'm sorry, Pa," he wept. "I couldn't help it. I tried to stop them, but they just took my leg away."

Pa shook his head slowly in silence.

"The field surgeon said I could keep it," cried Jem. "But Dr. Ludlow cut it off. It wasn't my fault, Pa. They tied me down. I couldn't do anything."

Pa stared at him. His face looked as sad as when he used to talk about his dead wife.

"Pa! I didn't lose it on purpose. It was an accident!"

The worst dream came night after night. It was the last battlefield. There were no sounds. It was a grim and silent pantomime. Jem saw the tall silhouette against the sunset over and over again. He could feel each pebble of the embankment under his elbows and the recoil of the rifle against his shoulder. Then he would awake from this nightmare and lie in his sweaty bed, surrounded by the echoes in the dark shadows of the hospital halls.

By the light of day it was easier to say he never could have known who was coming at him over the earthworks. Anybody would have figured, coming from that direction, it just had to be a Reb. He had thought Hank was already lying in the field behind him. He could think of all sorts of reasonable things. It didn't make him feel much better, but at least he didn't weep the way he did at night. But day or night, Jem just continued feeling that hollow, helpless anger.

Chapter Thirteen

SOUNDS OF WOMEN IN QUIET conversation gradually seeped into Jem's consciousness. His eyelids fluttered, but he couldn't see the speakers.

"I'm so glad you're here," said a scratchy old voice, "but I do worry about you."

"I'm not sure why," said a musical young voice. "I'm quite all right, you know."

Jem decided that neither woman was talking to him, so he stopped trying to open his eyes.

"Well, actually I'm worried about Miss Dix's rule," said the scratchy voice. "No woman under thirty years need apply to work in government hospitals."

"But I thought we agreed that I'm not actually applying for work, Aunt Ella. I'm here as your personal assistant."

"Sarah, the Good Lord knows that in my exhausted condition I need your assistance very much indeed, but sometimes I worry that someone will say we are defying the spirit of the rule."

"Dragon Dix is over sixty, and who knows what she intended as the spirit of the rule? Is anyone under thirty just a silly schoolgirl?"

Jem's eyes popped open, and he saw the two women standing across the aisle by the cot of the soldier from Illinois. One of them was a rivetingly attractive girl with peach-blush cheeks, hyacinth-blue eyes, and dark silky hair, parted in the middle and swept back behind her head.

"My dear," said the older woman, "as a very grown-up fifteen-year-old, you are rarely a silly schoolgirl. But I'm sure Miss Dorothea Dix made her rule after a great deal of serious consideration."

"And when you asked me to help you, Aunt Ella, you warned me that we might both get banished if we ignored that rule."

"Consider how much of themselves these boys have given for the country—for us, Sarah. I must stay and care for them."

"Even alone? Even if they banish me but not you?"

"I would have to go on, my dear girl. But the possibility keeps me awake for hours each night."

The two women moved on down the line of beds. Jem could still hear the sound of their voices but not the words. He watched Sarah as she went from one lethargic soldier to the next.

WHEN SHE WAS GONE, HE closed his eyes and slept again. First the old dreams came, and then a new one. He saw a vision of Hank lying in a meadow of wildflowers with two huge crows perched on his chest. Around him in the grass yellow hawkweed, orange devil's paintbrush, and purple vetch swayed in the summer breeze. A crow spread its ragged wings, and a black pinfeather spiraled down among the dancing flowers.

The crow cawed loudly, and Jem jolted awake to find a tiny old woman bending over his bandaged leg. Instead of a beak, she had a round wrinkled face that looked like a stale muffin. She cawed again and began picking at the bandage.

"Unh-ah!" gasped Jem after one especially vigorous tweak.

"Too much seepage here," crowed the little creature. "Needs a clean bandage, young man."

Jem stuffed a corner of his pillow between his teeth and clamped hard while the old woman yanked off the strips of bandage. Tears seeped between his tightly clenched eyelids as she sponged around the wound and began clumsily wrapping fresh bandages on his throbbing leg. When she was finally done, she hobbled away, muttering to herself. Jem lay for a long time, puffing like a steam engine, and at last his gasps subsided into labored breathing as the pain slowly diminished.

Shadows grew between the cots as evening crept into the hospital. Through his half-shut eyes Jem saw out-of-focus figures of orderlies and nurses softly drifting like blurred ghosts in the mist. When darkness closed in, the ominous peace of the chilly night swaddled him with its uneasy symphony of creaks and moans. He floated restlessly back and forth between the gloom of his waking thoughts and the horror of his recurrent nightmare, Hank's gangling silhouette against a hellish sunset. Finally, just before the pale dawn sent its hesitant tentacles of light along the hallways, Jem slipped into an exhausted slumber that lasted well into the morning.

HE WAS AWAKENED BY THE gentle touch of sunlight on his face. As he basked in the soothing warmth, he heard the violalike tones of a beautiful feminine voice. Rolling his head toward the music, he saw the girl named Sarah standing beside his bed. Jem would have thought it perfectly natural if golden wings had sprouted from her shoulders. He stared and she smiled, brushing a loose lock of hair from her forehead.

"I asked you a question."

"What was that, ma'am?"

"'Ma'am?'" She laughed. "Do you want to make me feel like an old lady? Call me Sarah. Or any other name you like, except ma'am. My question was, Who made such a bad job of bandaging your leg? A child could have done better."

"Yesterday a little old woman with a face like a withered apple came wobbling in here. Said the bandage needed a change, and she went right to it. Hurt like the Devil."

"I might have known. That was Miss Trudy. She doesn't seem to realize that she's half blind."

"I've spoken to her several times," said Aunt Ella, bustling up and placing a bowl of steaming water on the rickety wooden chair beside the bed. "I even offered to teach her how to do bandages. She replied that she knew enough to get along, thank you."

"Get along, indeed," Sarah retorted. "You would never think it to see this rats' nest."

Sarah and Aunt Ella started to undo Miss Trudy's handiwork. Jem watched Sarah until he had to clench his eyes, but the pain seemed much less than usual. The two women managed to be brisk and gentle at the same time. When they were finished, Sarah stood up straight and looked at Jem.

"You seem a little better," she said. "Would you like me to bring some paper next time so you can sit up and write a letter home?"

"No one to write to. My mother's dead. I don't know where my father is. Maybe my granddad made it home and maybe he didn't. Anyway, I'm scared to write to him, seeing I ran away from the farm when he asked me to look after it for him. I got to think he's tearing mad at me. He has a temper on him like thunder and lightning."

"Aren't there other family members or even friends who would like to hear from you?"

"There's no one else at home except maybe old Bertie, and she can't read," said Jem.

"Perhaps she would find someone to read your letter to her."

Jem rolled his head and looked away. "Uncle Milford can't read either."

"I'll bring paper next time anyway," she said, "and pen and ink. Just in case. Maybe you'll think of somebody. Now I must catch up with Aunt Ella."

As he watched Sarah hurry away down the aisle, Jem thought she seemed to be gliding a few inches above the floor.

THE NEXT DAY JEM'S EYES were open when Sarah and her aunt made their appearance. He watched them moving from soldier to soldier. When they reached his cot, Sarah stood beside him, smiling but with a worried look in her eyes.

"You seem a little peaked today," she said. "Did you sleep well?"

"No ma'am," replied Jem. "The dreams woke me up a lot."

"Please, I told you my name is Sarah. War dreams?"

"Hank."

"Who's Hank?" asked Sarah, hugging a bundle of fresh bandages as she seated herself on the chair beside Jem's bed.

"This won't get the day's work done," complained Aunt Ella, turning so abruptly that a small dollop of water sloshed from her bowl and splatted on the floor. "I'll just step across the aisle to start on that poor boy who's lost both his feet. But you really shouldn't play favorites. Don't linger, my dear."

"You were telling me about Hank," said Sarah, ignoring her aunt.

"He was my best friend."

"You say 'was' your friend. Did you lose him?"

"Oh yes. I lost him all right. He's dead."

"In the war?"

Jem paused, wondering just how to put his pain into words. Then he decided to slide over it and mumbled, "He was shot in the same charge that I was."

"My father and my oldest brother went off to war. They are both dead now, but from their letters I learned that Army friendships can be remarkably close. Do you think the bonds are made stronger by the risk, the fear of being wounded or killed?"

"Hank was more than a war friend. We were children together, knew each other since we learned to walk. Neither one of us had a blood brother, so we grew up like brothers. We joined the Army together. I've lost my brother."

Sarah gazed at the window for a moment, and the sun made tawny highlights in her dark hair. "Well, then, that must make it much more painful. Are you at the very bottom of grief? Oh dear! Foolish question. How could you not be deep down in those gloomy depths? Maybe such terrible pain can never be totally forgotten, but let's hope it becomes less intense in your mind as you get better. Then you might be able to look to your future again."

"I'll never do that. I can't."

"Never?" she said, scowling.

Jem felt sweat on his forehead and blurted, "I haven't told the whole story about Hank."

"Enough for me to think of you as brothers."

"I killed him, Sarah."

She gazed away again, took a quick breath, and turned back to Jem. "I thought you said he died in a charge."

"I was in the same charge, and I shot him."

"Surely you couldn't have done it on purpose, could you?"

"I thought he was a Confederate fixing to kill me," Jem whimpered.

"How absolutely terrible! But how on earth can you be blamed? Every soldier risks death in battle."

"Not from his best friend," wept Jem. He didn't care if she saw his tears.

"But the swift action of war is so unpredictable. I haven't been in battle myself, of course, but I have learned that war creates unexpected destruction and agony for everyone in it or near it, and even for many who are only innocent bystanders. Sometimes I think it doesn't matter who pulled the trigger once the dead are dead."

"Sometimes I feel like I should be dead, too."

"That's understandable," said Sarah. "But would your death bring Hank back to life? Besides, you have a life ahead of you."

"Not one that looks worth the trouble."

"But you're not dead yet. I think that's quite lucky."

"Lucky?" spat Jem. "What makes you think that? Who in blazes are you to call me lucky?"

"Well," she said tensely, "your leg looks to be healing nicely. You might have lost it, you know."

"I know," growled Jem. "Like you just said, I'm supposed to feel lucky. Lots of people told me I was lucky. I always got mad at them. I guess I can't stay mad at you, though. Nobody could."

"Aunt Ella can. But why on earth would you get angry with people who say you're lucky?"

"Because I'd be more lucky if I was dead."

Sarah gasped and then stood up, almost dropping her bundle of bandages. She gasped again and then fled after her aunt. Jem wanted to run after her and explain. But he couldn't think what words he would use. And he couldn't run anyway.

He stared up at the ceiling. Sarah had said he was lucky. So had Dr. Ludlow and the doctor in the field hospital. And Solomon. What else had Solomon said? "You just keep your mind on living. Somebody wanted for you to live." They just don't understand, thought Jem. Not a one of them can see that I plain don't deserve to live.

CHRISTMAS WAS A RATHER DREARY celebration for the wounded soldiers in the hospital, even for the men soon to be released. For those like Jem, who still had to look ahead to weeks of recovery, it was definitely a forlorn event. A few men had visits from nearby friends or relatives, and Jem held a faint hope that Sarah might visit, too, but she seemed to have disappeared without a trace, as though she had been a dream. None of Jem's actual dreams were as beautiful as Sarah, however, and deep down he knew he had frightened her off with his talk of death.

The staff tried to bring in some good cheer with wreaths and bunches of holly. Children came in small groups to sing carols, but they were uneasy at the sight of so many injured soldiers. Their uncertain voices sounded fragile, and their worried faces lacked the brightness of the season. "The First Nowell" was a dismal diversion for Jem. The second line about "certain poor shepherds" pulled his mind far away from the Christmas story. He thought not of shepherds but of dead soldiers "in fields where they lay."

Especially, he imagined Hank lying on a Rebel embankment, a stiff corpse in the cold night.

ON A GLOOMY DAWN IN mid-January, Jem listened to sleet rattling against the windows and wondered why he had not deserted on the chilly night that the thought had occurred to him while on picket duty. If he had run, at least he would not have shot Hank, and if he had been caught, he would have been shot but at least he wouldn't be lying here thinking he did not deserve to live.

The sleet continued all day long. Jem brooded until dusk over scenes of the incredible human cost of the war. As night closed in, the parade of visions intensified. He could not erase the sight of Donovan's maggoty face or forget the sickening stench of the corpses at Spotsylvania. He knew he would have endless nightmares of the appalling slaughter of men at the Battle of the Crater.

One of the most vivid memories that plagued Jem that night and throughout the chill of winter was the image of the girl crying while her family's barn burned. What had she done to deserve the hardship that must have followed the burning? Was that the cost of freeing the slaves? Was that the price of preserving the unitedness of the United States? Was such hellish destruction fair? How did you excuse all that with the few words Hank had uttered while they sat watching a spectacular mortar bombardment at Cold Harbor: "Who's to say what's fair? It's war."

Chapter Fourteen

ᴏɴ ᴏɴᴇ ᴏꜰ ᴛʜᴇ ꜰᴇᴡ bright days in February, when icicles were melting into a curtain of glittering drops in the hospital window, a shadow moved hesitantly across Jem's hospital cot. His eyes blinked open to the sight of Sarah, standing in the sunlight. When she saw that he was awake, she sat down nervously on the edge of the creaking chair.

"Your color looks much healthier," she said quietly.

"Oh? Hello, Sarah," said Jem, sitting up. "You've been away such a long time, I feared you were gone for good."

"I see she's still at it," Sarah said, with an unexpectedly sharp note of exasperation in her usually mellow voice.

"Who's still at what?" said Jem, his eyes opening wider.

"Miss Trudy, of course. She's done your leg in her usual haphazard way. I'd know that work anywhere."

"I guess there weren't many other ladies around. But I sure wish you'd been here. You did a lot better job of it."

"I couldn't be here, but I rather hoped someone other than Trudy might have tended to you. I've been looking after Aunt Ella these past weeks. She's still so exhausted she can't get out of bed, and she worries too much. Today she seems a bit more lively and cheerful, so I thought I might leave her, just for a little while, although I must admit I was sort of afraid to."

"Afraid to leave your aunt? I can believe it," said Jem.

"No. Afraid you wouldn't be here."

"Where would I go? Where could I go?"

116

"You said you'd be more lucky if you were dead. That really frightened me. I've seen quite a few soldiers die here, and I lost my father and my oldest brother to this horrible war, but I'm still not used to death. My father died after First Bull Run. Manassas. They amputated his leg, but he died anyway. My brother died at Chickamauga, out in Tennessee. I wasn't supposed to know how, but I overheard Aunt Ella explaining it to her friend Mrs. Potter. A shell blew his head off. I couldn't sleep for weeks after hearing that."

"Makes a person mad," said Jem. "You wonder why those Rebels won't just give up and call it quits."

"Both sides should call it quits," said Sarah bitterly. "Father was a Confederate with Stonewall Jackson's Virginians, and my brother was in the Union Army of the Cumberland. Every day I pray it's all over before my two younger brothers are old enough to volunteer. They think their father and brother are heroes. I'm not sure if they know which side they'd fight for, but they can hardly wait to march off to glory."

"You can tell them that glory is a fool's dream. My best friend and I were going to become heroes on the battlefield. We were going to come home to heroes' welcomes and sit back in glory for the rest of our days. What really happened was we shot up a lot of healthy farm boys like ourselves. We got real good at it. Then I got shot up myself. And I shot my best friend. You can tell your brothers that glory's not all it's made out to be."

"I wish you could tell them."

"Well, Sarah, maybe when I get out of here and start my own life, I could visit them and explain why they won't find what they're hoping for in this war."

117

"Start your own life? That's a new outlook for you."

"It's been a long winter. Plenty of time to think on things. In fact, there hasn't been a whole lot else I could do except for limping around this bed once a day, leaning on that chair. Hurts like blazes, but back in bed when the pain lets up some, there I am, thinking again."

"About what?"

"You and a lot of other people calling me lucky and an old black man telling me someone wanted real bad for me to live."

"Someone? Meaning God?"

"Maybe Solomon meant it that way, but I took it to mean Hank."

"Hank?"

"Sure. He had to know I was the one who shot him, and he had to know he would never survive that minié ball in his stomach. Too much bleeding. But Hank handed me his last bit of life with the strength he used to twist that canteen-strap tourniquet onto my leg. It was like he left me a message: 'Live, Jem-boy, live. For both of us.'"

"Live," said Sarah quietly. "Jem-boy? Was that what he called you?"

"Yes. And back home so did my pa and my granddad. But the blacks called me Mister Little-James, because they called Granddad Mister Big-James."

"Jem-boy," Sarah repeated. "Little-James. I don't think either name suits you now. I'll call you by your given name, James. Yes, James sounds right, and I doubt that Hank would mind. I hope he would be happy that your life has survived such a terrible mistake."

"The war's been nothing but a whole mess of mistakes, and the biggest mistake of all is the war itself."

Sarah put a hand lightly on Jem's arm. "Yes," she whispered. "I think you're right."

ALTHOUGH IT HAD SEEMED TO Jem that the great day would never come, Dr. Ludlow finally decided it was time for him to stand up and try some experimental walking without the support of the chair.

"Be careful, son," he said. "Just stand up slowly. Here. Use this cane for support. That's right."

"Thank you, sir," said Jem uneasily.

"Take short steps like a little child just learning to walk. Tomorrow you can try walking along the aisle a few steps, but don't go far and be sure you have a nurse alongside to steady you so you won't fall on your face. Does it hurt?"

"Yes sir," said Jem, "but not too much, nothing like it used to."

"It'll likely twinge now and then for the rest of your life, such as when there's a change in the weather. I think you'll need the cane."

"For the rest of my life?"

"Most probably," said Dr. Ludlow. "In any case you're out of the Army for a long time to come. Now, let's see what you can do."

A few small uncertain steps were all Jem could manage on the first try. Flames of pain shot through his wounded thigh, but he wasn't going to admit it to Dr. Ludlow or anyone else. He took a deep breath and shuffled to the foot of the bed, paused for another rest, then turned to cross past the end and stopped at the other corner to rest again. He felt as though he had just completed a twenty-mile march with a sixty-pound pack on his back, but he also felt elated to be just a bit more mobile than he had leaning on the chair.

"Good work for the first try," said the doctor. "You're a lucky young man."

"I didn't think so for a long time," said Jem, "but today I really feel it. Yes sir, I am a lucky soldier."

"Now get back into bed. Try for more distance tomorrow. Then try a couple of times a day, always with a nurse. You don't need me anymore, and the hospital needs your bed, so get to work."

SARAH WAS THE ONLY ONE Jem wanted helping him. It wasn't hard to arrange that, as Aunt Ella was still at home and Miss Trudy looked as though she could offer no more support than a small rag doll. The first day Jem and Sarah shuffled along the aisle past nine beds, from which some of the occupants raised feeble cheers of encouragement.

The next day they passed fourteen beds, which inspired Jem to remark, "Real soon now I'll be heading back to Gaithersburg."

"That's something to look forward to," Sarah said. "It wouldn't be much of a trip when you're fully recovered, but keep in mind that'll still be a while yet. Who knows when you'll be comfortable on a horse, and you're certainly not ready to walk such a distance."

"In the old days," said Jem, "I could have walked it in one long day or done it by horse in less than half a day, but right now I don't even own a horse. I've been thinking I could walk it if I went slow, just a few miles a day, take a few days to do the whole jaunt."

"You'd freeze to death! And besides, where would you stay at night?"

"Sarah, it isn't that the Frederick Pike is some kind of wilderness trail. Rockville's got more than one tavern, and

120

there's farms along the way where I know folks would let me sleep in their barns or cowsheds."

"And what if your bad leg gives out?"

"I'll just have to hope it doesn't. Look, Sarah, the way I figure it, I don't have any choice."

"Maybe you do. Aunt Ella's house is a big old thing. I'll ask her if you might use a spare room for a week or two."

"I don't think she likes me, Sarah."

"That's just her way, James. She likes you more than you know."

SARAH EASILY PERSUADED AUNT ELLA that Jem had no other place to regain his strength before attempting the trip home to Gaithersburg. Jem moved in, and every day Sarah took time from her hospital work to walk with him in the wintry air. March came in like a lion of ice bellowing bone-freezing roars. In fact, the fourth was so cold and windy that Sarah wanted to call off the daily walk, but Jem insisted on going out, because it was Inauguration Day and he wanted to hear President Lincoln's speech.

"We'll freeze like statues if we stand still," said Sarah, "and anyway, his words will be blown away by the wind. We can read the complete speech later in the newspaper."

"When the military ballots were issued," Jem replied, "I couldn't vote because I wasn't old enough, but I would have voted for Lincoln. Most soldiers did, even some who fought under General McClellan at the beginning of the war and who liked him and might have voted for him. They voted for Abe Lincoln instead. I've just got to hear his speech, Sarah."

They bundled themselves up in heavy overcoats with two scarves each, one around the neck and another tied across the face and over the head to protect the ears. Jem tried to swing his cane jauntily, and they walked as briskly as his shaky leg would allow. When they came in sight of the Capitol, they stood still for a moment to gaze in wonder at the colossal bronze statue that only that morning had been hoisted onto the pillared cupola that crowned the ornate dome.

"That's a mighty tall lady," said Jem. "I wonder who she is."

"That's *Freedom*," replied Sarah. "I read in the newspaper that she was designed by a man named Thomas Crawford, and she's nearly twenty feet tall."

"Well, I guess twenty feet could be just about right for *Freedom*. She has a big job."

In spite of the piercingly cold weather, a large number of people were milling around in front of the wooden platform that had been built on the Capitol steps. The crowd pushed Jem and Sarah tightly forward as everyone squeezed closer to see the tall president, minus his usual stovepipe hat, step up to the lectern with his dark hair fluttering above his high forehead. When he began to speak, a few of his words were lost in the gusting wind, but Jem and Sarah were able to hear most of the speech.

Afterward, as they walked back to Aunt Ella's, they talked about the president's message.

"'With malice toward none, with charity for all,'" Jem quoted.

"I like the way Mr. Lincoln puts his words together," said Sarah. "And James, I'm very glad you insisted that we come to hear him."

THE NEXT DAY IN AUNT ELLA'S back parlor, warmed by a potbellied stove, Jem and Sarah sat together on a love seat to browse through the speech printed in the *Washington Star*. As they read side by side, their shoulders were gently pressed together, and Jem wondered if the tingling warmth he felt was caused by President Lincoln's speech or Sarah's touch.

"'A just and lasting peace,'" read Sarah softly. "Peace," she murmured, almost as if to herself. "I've ached for that ever since my father died. If we all worked very hard at peace, I wonder if we could make this the last war on earth."

Jem was already lost in his own thoughts. He knew he felt drawn to this wonderful person who, though she had the fresh charm of a girl, sometimes showed the seasoned wisdom of a woman. He admired these two aspects of Sarah in a warm and longing way that he had never felt toward anyone before. He supposed the warmth must be Sarah herself, but he knew the longing came from within him, because first he had to go to Gaithersburg and then maybe other places he hadn't even planned on yet. He would have to leave Sarah for a while.

"But I'll be coming back to see you one day," he said abruptly.

She looked up, perplexed. "But you haven't gone anywhere," she said, laughing. "Or are you already off in some world of your own?"

"Oh no," he said in mild embarrassment. "I only meant that I have to go on to Gaithersburg soon. And I've been thinking lately that I should see more of the country before I settle down."

"But you can't travel until the weather's warmer."

"I'll have to be leaving right soon," he asserted. "There's so much to do in Gaithersburg before I go anywhere else.

I've got to see how the farm is, how my grandfather is, how Bertie and Uncle Milford are, and maybe most of all find out where my father is."

"I'm sure you'll find your father."

"Then I'll be coming back here."

Quietly, Sarah replied, "I'd like that."

Chapter Fifteen

"YOU GOT TO BE THE thinkingest man I ever traveled with," the heavyset teamster said in his deep, rough-edged voice. Then he spat a long squirt of tobacco juice at the muscular brown rumps of the two Clydesdale workhorses laboring just beyond his dusty boots. He missed. Slowly, patiently, six broad-hoofed horses, their feathery white fetlocks sometimes invisible in the early-morning ground mist, were hauling eight tons of dry goods stowed snugly in the curved hull of a Conestoga wagon. At the moment of the teamster's surly comment, they were rumbling through the just-awakening town of Rockville.

"You takin' an extra snooze?" asked the teamster.

"I was just thinking about Mr. Lincoln's speech," Jem replied. He was also thinking about Sarah, but he wasn't going to mention that to the reeky bear sitting next to him.

"Last week?" said the man. "The Inaugurary? It was kinda puny, if you ask me. I've heard lots better at a Fourth of July picnic."

Jem reflected that he hadn't asked the teamster's opinion, but just to be civil he replied, "It was short."

"That's what I mean. Puny. Not near enough fireworks."

"Seems to me," said Jem, "fireworks was just what he didn't want. 'That this mighty scourge of war may speedily pass away' was what I thought he was asking for."

"Depends on which side you're on," growled the teamster.

"I figure we must all be wanting 'a just and lasting peace,' no matter whose side we're on."

"Maybe," replied the teamster, "maybe, if it's just you and me jawing about the war. But folks expect a little blood and thunder when they crowd up to hear speechifying."

"Maybe some folks," said Jem grimly.

"Soldier folks like you got to have glorious memories. You was in the war, wasn't you?"

"I was," said Jem. "That's how I got this game leg. But I'm here to tell you, mister, there is nothing glorious about it."

The teamster glanced at him curiously and then spat toward the Clydesdales again. As he watched the fellow cut another plug and push it into his mouth, Jem thought that if a squirt of tobacco juice ever did hit the genial, plodding animals, most likely they would take no notice.

"Gaithersburg," said the teamster. "We'll be hauling through it directly. Where did you want to get off?"

"Big farm on the left. It's just up on the next hill."

"That one? I don't believe there's been anyone there, oh, maybe a year and a half now. Don't look worked. Not much hope of a job there, I figure. You sure you don't want to travel on a spell?"

"I'll take my chances."

"And I'll miss my chance to hear some good war stories."

An arching amber glob splatted on the rump of the left rear horse. The teamster grinned. A tiny brown trickle appeared at the corner of his mouth and began to dribble into the bristles on his chin. "Charity for all," thought Jem. Even for this fellow here. If he had to travel far with him, he guessed he'd need the patience of a Clydesdale.

"So here's your big chance, soldier boy," said the teamster as the wagon creaked to halt. Jem swung awkwardly down, favoring his bad leg.

"Thanks," he said.

126

"Don't mention it."

Jem looked up. "Well, I will mention one thing."

"Yeah?"

"If you'd been in just one battle, you wouldn't want to hear anybody's war stories."

"If you b'lieve it's so."

"I know it's so," said Jem evenly. "And most likely you wouldn't feel like telling any of your own, either."

"Well, good luck to you anyway, soldier."

JEM STOOD WATCHING THE HUGE creaking wagon lumbering slowly up the hill until it disappeared over the crest. Then he turned and set out to limp up the weed-edged farm road he knew so well. The house did look empty, and the paint was peeling off the veranda. Nevertheless, Jem felt a sense of relief at coming home. It didn't last long. As he got closer to the house, he began to feel spooky. He was glad it was bright morning and not midnight. If there were strangers living here, he might not like meeting them.

At home before the war Jem had never used the front door much, and he decided not to use it now. He went quietly around the side, where he had run breathlessly the day the foragers had burned the barn. Moving as slowly as a stalking cat, he flicked his eyes back and forth, looking for any sign of motion. He wanted to see some sort of life but was afraid of finding something unpleasant. When he reached the corner, he heard a familiar bark. Teddy was running hard when Jem turned the corner. The dog almost knocked him down. Then he started feverishly licking Jem's outstretched hand.

"Hush up, you old fleabag," called out a voice from the past. "What kind of mess you getting in— Land sakes! Mist'

Little-James! You ain't a ghost, now, is you? No, not in broad daytime. Lordy, you like to scared this old black girl into her grave. It is you, ain't it, honey?"

Bertie and Uncle Milford had been sitting on the back porch steps, warming their skinny old shanks in the sun. Slowly, Bertie began to stand, and then she wobbled forward.

"It's me all right, Bertie. No ghost, but I almost was."

"Lord 'a' mercy, Mist' Little-James. We near about gave you up for dead. Thank the Lord you's preserved." She flung her kindling-wood arms around Jem in a bony hug. "God done carried you through the fire," she said, weeping.

"I guess He did," blurted Jem, himself weeping enough to flood Seneca Creek, "with a lot of help from Solomon. He found me on the field and carried me to a hospital. I begged him to stay with me but he refused. Said he had to get on with his new life and couldn't ever come back here."

"Bless you, Mist' Little-James, I knew Solomon wouldn't be back when he left. Now, stand there and let me look at you, child. Well, you done grown some, but you need fattening, Mist' Little-James. Only you're not rightly Mist' Little-James anymore." Bertie's smile wreathed a hundred wrinkles on the dark leather of her ancient face. "You's Mis-ter James now," she said fervently. "Onh-honh . . . Mister James."

As THEY ENTERED THE DARKENED back parlor, Bertie was clutching Jem's elbow. "Mist' Big-James," she called out in her thin old voice, "look who's here. Look who done come home." She turned and whispered, "I surely do hope he knows you, Mist' James, but he might not. Some days he's just not right in his head."

128

Jem stared at the shadowy scarecrow lying on the makeshift cot in the gloomy room. At one time it could have been Granddad, he thought, but it sure didn't show the grand old style. He could just make out a gray face in the soft light. The eyes were closed like thin parchment stretched over a couple of bird eggs. The brittle lids fluttered and then opened. The hazel eyes were Granddad's, all right.

"Jem-boy," he croaked, like a raven in the tall oaks. "Thought . . . we . . . lost you."

"The Good Lord done carried your boy through the fire," cried Bertie. "'Deed He has, Mist' Big-James. Through the fire."

"Jem-boy. . . . Tomorrow . . . we'll make . . . a . . . a new boat."

His eyes closed slowly, and the raspy breathing became more regular. The set of his face seemed to say the interview was over. Everyone was dismissed. Jem and Bertie left the room.

"I don't rightly know what it is," said Bertie as she dropped another stick of wood into the stove. "'Deed I don't. He's been getting worser and worser all this past winter. He got to lookin' poorly back at cider-making time. I recollect the mornings were feelin' frosty-like and Milford was getting the barrels ready. Seemed like your grandpa had no heart for it. Now, you know that wasn't right, Mist' James. 'Deed it wasn't. Mist' Big-James was always most particular how that applejack got along in the barrel. Studied it every day, like he did most things on the farm."

"Oh, I do recollect," said Jem, creaking back and forth in the familiar old rocking chair. "Whatever it is, I wonder how it came on."

"I believe it likely begun before last autumn, 'most a year before. Only it come on so slow, we didn't see it for a while.

Mist' James, I believe it goes back to losing the livestock and the barn."

"But he wasn't here when the barn burned."

"No, Mist' James, he didn't rightly see the flames, but he saw the ashes about a week after you went to the Army. Kind of took the starch out of him."

"Used to take a whole lot more than that to slow him down. Days gone by, he'd have had a new barn up before a fellow could finish whistling 'The Battle Hymn of the Republic.'"

"Days gone by, you'd be right, Mist' James. Yes, indeed. But you know, he come home on foot and empty-handed."

"I never did want to think he might have fooled us all and up and joined the Confederate Army."

"You know he couldn't ever do that, 'cause Mist' Thomas went for the Union Army and somebody had to look after the farm. No, Mist' James, he was gone for extra supplies, just like he said. He always was a good provider. Only he couldn't provide so much anymore, but he still done his best, helping us find enough food to scratch on through the winter. And last summer when General Jubal Early come through here, foragers took near about every last thing left."

"Didn't he tell them he was Confederate?"

"'Deed he did, Mist' James. He done that, all right. But them Rebel boys needed food worse than we did. And with General Early setting up his headquarters right here in the dining room, seemed like we had to give him just about any little thing he wanted."

"And I guess they told him that if he was a true Confederate, he had to support the war effort."

"Mm-hmm. That's right, Mist' James. And when the Rebels was gone again, we was mighty lucky there was enough left for us to scrounge a little bit for the winter. We could have starved."

"Bertie, I believe this war's been terrible for everyone, no matter which side they're on. I guess the next question is, what can we do about Granddad?"

"He needs doctoring, Mist' James. He's just slipping away."

"Where is there a doctor, Bertie? Even before I left, old Doc Goodman went to Washington to look after wounded. Or did he come back?"

"No, he didn't come back, Mist' James. We'll just have to doctor on him ourselves. I expect I've got as many cures as any doctor and some he wouldn't know about. I done tried a few already, but ain't nothin' worked yet. I reckon it's time to try my granny's melancholy broth. I'll boil up a pot directly."

Jem had no idea what went into that broth. No one ever got a recipe out of Bertie. She tried to spoon the broth into Granddad, but a lot of it never got in. At night she dozed in a chair beside his bed. If he seemed to be awake, she would sing the mockingbird lullaby Jem remembered from his own childhood. It was a peaceful and soothing song, but it did not seem to do much for Granddad and it did not calm Jem as it had when he was little. He had gone through too much to return to those golden days. He remembered the exhausting marches and the long hospital nights when he had longed to be back on the farm, but now that he was home, he felt he could not stay indefinitely. Sooner or later he would move on.

FOR SEVERAL NIGHTS JEM LAY awake, wondering how he might describe this new restlessness to Bertie and what sort of convincing words he could find to explain the problem to Granddad. He would ponder for hours in the solemn darkness before sleep finally overcame him. One gray dawn he was startled to find Bertie clawing at his shoulder.

"Mist' James, come quick. He's leaving. Bound to be soon now. I must have dropped off, and next I know he's calling for your grandma, dead these years, but real soft. 'Deed if I didn't know Miz Eveline's name, I couldn't have made out what he was saying."

Jem ran as fast as his game leg would allow, down the stairs and into the back parlor. Bertie was slower. Each step on the stairway was a separate effort for her.

"Jem-boy," said Granddad, sounding a little bit like old times, "bend over so's I don't have to shout."

"Here I am, Granddad," said Jem, kneeling beside the bed.

"Few items of business. . . . My shaving stand . . . it's for you, Jem-boy."

"You'll be using it soon enough."

"Don't think so, boy. . . . Bertie told me how you kept it from the foragers. . . . Pass it on to the oldest boy in your litter when you have one. . . . Tell him your story . . . and give him the gold watch that's in the left-hand drawer."

"That's a ways off yet, Granddad."

"Your time will come . . . sooner than you think, Jem-boy. . . . One more thing. . . . You got to tend to the farm. . . . Mind the farm, boy."

"I can mind it until Pa comes back."

"Your pa's . . . gone. . . . Yankee anyway. . . . Him and his railroad . . . as good as dead. . . . He is dead. You were too young to know . . . what you were doing. . . . But . . . you're home now."

"I guess I could do it," said Jem. He figured he must have soaked up a lot of farming ways as a little tadpole riding in the buggy beside Granddad. Then, of course, he had worked at just about every job there was on the farm. But he would have to put off traveling, at least for a while. "I'm here now, Grandpa."

"I know, Jem-boy. . . . I been waiting . . . long time. . . . It's your home. . . . You belong . . . belong here. . . . Been . . . waiting. . . . Now . . . I'm ready. . . ." For a few long minutes a rhythmical rasping sound filled the gray room, then only the chirping of birds outside, greeting the new day.

Jem put his head on Granddad's still and silent chest and began to weep. He thought he'd seen enough soldiers die to have no tears left. But this was his granddad. He had to cry for him. Or were the tears for himself? Then Bertie was hugging him. It reminded him of a time years and years back. She had dropped a bundle of clean wet washing in the dirt to hold him when he'd fallen and hurt his head.

"Now, just you hush yourself, honey. Your granddaddy's crossed the river now. He's feeling tall and strong like he used to. Yes, Mist' Big-James is singing with the angels, glory all around. Don't fret yourself, honey. He's going to be just fine."

A hot orange wave swept through Jem. The old anger had returned. He ran from the parlor and through the kitchen, and half tumbled down the back porch steps. He stood in the backyard, puffing like a locomotive. Then he dragged off into the neglected cornfield and limped up and down among the old and whispering dead stalks. The ears had been picked last August for human food, but there were no animals needing fodder, so no one had bothered to cut the six-foot-high corn plants and bundle them into the customary sheaves. Stopping at last, Jem looked down at his bare feet in the cool rich soil. He was still wearing his nightshirt, and Teddy was licking his shins. He hadn't noticed the dog tagging along. And he hadn't noticed that his leg was hurting like old times. He sat down clumsily.

"Well, Teddy," Jem said, "here it is. Granddad's gone. No one else to run the farm. It's up to us, old pup. Won't be easy. No sir. But I told him I'd take care of it. Think you can do your share?"

Teddy licked the tears and sweat from Jem's face.

Chapter Sixteen

ON AN UNUSUALLY WARM MORNING in the last days of March, Bertie and Jem started working on the kitchen garden. Jem was savoring the rich, fresh smell of each spadeful of earth he dug up. The warm spring sun on his back persuaded him to rest a moment. He stood and slung the spade onto his right shoulder. He remembered another spring morning, only a year ago, when his shoulder had supported an Austrian rifle. Rather the spade than the rifle for sure, he thought, but spring would be halfway into summer before a man could finish turning over the sod with a spade in the big fields for wheat and corn. He needed the plow for that job. But the plow's wooden handles had burned off in the fire, and anyway there were no horses or even a mule to pull it. They needed some livestock. Except for a few chickens, Teddy was the only animal on the farm. Cows and horses would be better off with a barn to live in. The hay to feed them in winter had to be stored in a loft.

"Fixing to take a holiday?" called Bertie as she bent over some knotted twine she was stretching to mark a row for planting beans.

"Thinking about barns, Bertie. I have to figure how to build us one."

"We doing fine just getting going again, Mist' James. We got no field hands, just you and me and Milford, and no livestock to speak of. I don't see a big hurry-up for a barn. You could wait till next winter to be studying barns."

"No, Bertie. Without a barn it's not really a farm. Seems

as if those foragers burned the heart clean out of it. I don't want to wait until winter."

"You're a real man now," cackled Bertie in delight. "'Deed you is. You're going to go and do whatever you've a mind to do. You know what you got to do," she said. "You just go on about your man business."

A loud bark came from the pile of dry dead leaves where Teddy had been nested asleep in the sun. As soon as they looked, he was off across the yard and halfway down the driveway. A tattered and scrawny stranger was approaching slowly, cautiously. Jem felt suddenly alert and very uneasy. What would that tired old bag of bones want? Food? A bed? A job? What if they couldn't give him what he wanted? Would he try to take something by force? Jem thought maybe a rifle would be pretty comforting after all, just lying over there in the grass where he could grab it in a hurry.

The skeleton figure wore a dark slouch hat and a baggy military tunic so faded and dusty, it was impossible to guess what the original color had been. His left sleeve was empty and pinned up on itself. Teddy had stopped barking and was now exuberantly running in wide circles.

"Praise the Lord!" rasped Bertie. "Another lost soul done come through the fire."

Jem looked at Bertie and then back at the figure. He dropped the spade and started running. He didn't care how much the leg hurt. The weary scarecrow began a slow shuffling jog toward him. They met and then, too choked to say anything, hugged for a long time.

"Hugging's kind of lopsided with only one arm," said Pa.

LATE INTO THE NIGHT, FATHER and son recounted their experiences to each other. When he had returned to the war, Pa

136

had been attached to General Franz Sigel's staff in the Shenandoah Valley. Sigel, a German immigrant, desperately needed officers who could train new soldiers, but Pa was soon captured in a fierce little skirmish near Winchester. His badly shattered left arm was amputated by a Confederate surgeon, and he was sent to Libby Prison in Richmond.

"We heard terrible things about Confederate prisons," said Jem. "Used to say it would be better to get killed than captured."

"Almost," replied Pa. "More than a thousand Union officers crammed into six dingy rooms in an old warehouse, chandlery for ship supplies. Ropes and canvas and such. Stank to high heaven from bad sanitation."

"And not much to eat?"

"A few dried beans and a handful of cornmeal each day, but I'd have to say that wasn't too much worse than what the Rebel soldiers got to eat."

"Sounds like starvation to me," said Jem.

"Well, it made hundreds of us sick, that's for sure. Dysentery and fever, diarrhea beyond belief. It's a scary sight to see your friends with their gums bleeding and their teeth falling out from scurvy. Only a matter of time before my own teeth would have started to loosen up, but I had the good fortune to get exchanged for a Confederate officer before that could happen."

"Officers or enlisted men, I hear the Confeds generally treat all their prisoners like animals, worse even. If a farmer was to treat his livestock that way, he'd go broke in a season."

"Fruits of war, Jem-boy. From what I hear, Union prisons aren't any better. Folks don't like to talk about it much, but I picked up a rumor we're running a real hellhole up in Elmira, New York."

A slight breath of air wafted into the room, and the two men watched in silence as a fluttering candle dripped wax onto the dining table. When the flame straightened itself, Jem began to describe his own war experiences. He was matter-of-fact in his account of training at Camp Cass but became more dramatic in recounting the Battle of the Wilderness. His most vivid tale was about the foraging episode when Sergeant Evans had ordered Hank and Jem to burn the barn. In flat tones he recounted how he had left the task to Hank, but tears sprang to his eyes when he told of the girl who had stood near the blaze, weeping and watching her family's livelihood go up in flames.

At the end, however, he found it extremely difficult to talk about the last charge. He told the story in vague phrases with long silences, and Pa was mostly silent, too, although he reacted with a wordless cry at Jem's wounding and a louder one at Hank's shooting. After pausing a moment and then heaving a deep sigh of relief, Jem pressed on to a brisk description of his hospital stay and ended by speaking warmly of Sarah.

PA AND JEM SLEPT HARD that night and on into the morning, until they were awakened by the delicious smell of bacon frying in a skillet. It was an aroma that had not drifted through the halls of the old farmhouse since before the foragers had burned down the barn. Only Bertie knew by what mysterious and miraculous means she had acquired the meat, and she wasn't telling. The important thing was that it tasted far better than the barreled salt pork of Army cuisine.

"Jem-boy, have you seen any of my letters around the house?" asked Pa, as Bertie placed a stack of flapjacks on his plate. "I couldn't find any when I took a quick look in Granddad's desk and the dresser in his bedroom."

"No," said Jem. "But then I haven't been looking for any letters."

"Well, I suppose a lot of them were hardly worth saving," Pa remarked. "Turned out some messy ones before I figured out how to manage writing materials with only one hand. Didn't get replies either. But I always held on to the hope that folks here might know my whereabouts, and even if I was only rotting away in a Confederate prison, at least someone could believe I was alive."

Bertie left the room hastily, muttering, "Coffee's like to burn."

"Whenever you're ready, I'll help you do a thorough search of the whole house," said Jem. "One of us ought to save a few war notes."

"Didn't you write any letters?"

"No, Pa. Sorry to say. I left the farm to go looking for you and glory, and I didn't leave any messages behind either. Bertie knew I was going away, but she didn't know where I'd enlist or where I'd be sent. I wanted it that way, because I was afraid that if Granddad came home and found I had run away, he'd be so mad he'd have me tracked down and brought back."

Bertie returned to the dining room with a pot of coffee. "He was mad, all right," she said. "Oh yes. Mad as a wet hen. But not at you, Mist' James. He was mad at Mist' Thomas, real mad." From her apron pocket she pulled out a small bundle of paper tied up with twine and laid it by Pa's plate. "They ain't all here, Mist' Thomas. When he got the first one, Mist' Big-James didn't even open it. He threw it in the cookstove in the kitchen. Burned right fast, it did. Mist'

Big-James says, 'I don't care who he is, I ain't gonna read trash from a Yankee turncoat,' and he burned another letter, too, but I done slipped the rest behind the flour bin. Couldn't read them, so they went clean out of my head till you recollected me."

Silence settled on the room while Jem untied the frayed twine. Intently, he watched as Pa shuffled slowly through the letters, studying each and then carefully placing them one by one across the table as though playing an obscure and personal game of cards. He did not open any of them. Finally, he sighed deeply, piled the letters, held the bundle awkwardly in his one hand, tapped it on the table twice to align the edges, and handed it to Jem to tie up again.

"Come on," said Pa, rising from the table. "It's high time we got out there to study the barn situation."

He led the way to the back door. As they went through the kitchen, he paused, picked up a stove-lid handle, and inserted it in the little hole in the surface of one of the round cast-iron lids. He lifted it, peered in thoughtfully at the few small tongues of flame flickering among the glowing red coals, then placed the lid down beside the open hole in the stove top. Pa took the bundle of letters from Jem, dropped it onto the fire, and clanked the lid back into its resting place.

OUTSIDE THE BACK DOOR, PA took a walking stick from the small collection that Granddad had always kept leaning in a corner of the porch. At the barn site the warm spring sunshine made the charred timbers and black charcoal scattered in the grass seem darkly iridescent. Pa poked at a burned board with his walking stick. He flipped the board over and then looked up, squinting around at the outline of the barn's large and lonely footprint in the meadow.

"Granddad figured out the best place on the property to build a barn. I don't think we could do any better. Might as well rebuild her right here. We'll have to see if there's any seasoned lumber lying around the wood lot. Can't build with green wood, can we?"

"No," said Jem softly. He was gazing distantly at the Frederick Pike, where it crested a hill in the direction of Washington.

"But," said Pa, "we can't wait through the winter for fresh-cut wood to season. If we don't have our own good lumber, we'll have to go looking for it somewhere else."

Jem continued to stare down the pike. "Mr. Fulks," he mumbled.

"Old Man Fulks at the general store? Well, yes, I suppose. I know he has a huge wood lot, and he might have some lumber yet, if it didn't get requisitioned by somebody's Army. I'd imagine he'd ask a pretty price for it, though. Do you suppose he might give it to us on credit?"

"I suppose," muttered Jem.

"Yes, I imagine he would," said Pa. "He's a businessman and he drives a hard bargain, but he's fair. Now, as to the building. We won't change the location, but I think we might improve on the interior design." With the tip of the walking stick he began to draw architectural lines in the ashes. "Now, I was thinking that if we build the horse stalls over there, we'd be making better use of the space, and then over here . . . Jem-boy, you soaking any of this up?"

"What? Oh sure, Pa. We won't change the location of the horse stalls."

"You weren't even listening, were you? That's a hundred and eighty degrees opposite of what I was saying. Your mind must be somewhere else."

"Sorry, Pa. My head must have been grazing out in Big Meadow or someplace."

"I'd guess farther than that," said Pa, smiling. "Maybe as far away as Washington, D.C."

Chapter Seventeen

⌒⌒⌒

IN THE EVENING AFTER SUPPER, Pa and Jem stood at the top of the back porch steps. The last week of March had been unusually warm. Soft earthy smells, hinting of spring, wafted gently on the night air, and down in the swampy place near the creek a few early peepers raised their small, intense voices in a shrill roundelay.

"Pretty soon we'll be smelling those lilacs out there," said Pa. "Do you remember the last time we listened to a night song as fervent as those peepers?"

"It wasn't spring peepers that time," replied Jem. "It was the katydids chirping, 'Katy did, Katy didn't.' You were going back to the war next day, and I got confused and thought you figured those bugs were telling us things would never be the same again."

"Even if our conversation slipped a cog that time, you could say your katydids were right."

"I guess I learned that the hard way, and I'm not through yet."

"Well," said Pa, "at least you got back home."

"Maybe that's the hardest part of all."

"How's that?"

"First off, I have got to visit Hank's ma."

"Jem-boy. I figured you'd already done that."

"I should have, Pa, only I can't think what to say to her. I hate the idea of telling her I shot her son, and I think that if I do tell her, she'll only feel worse than she does already."

"You've got yourself a tough one, son. The War Department must have informed her of Hank's death long before you came home, so she's done a lot of grieving. Maybe if you just go visit with her, you can judge for yourself if she needs to know more about how he died. I can't tell you what to say, but you'd best not put off the visit."

"I can't put if off much longer anyway. It's part of the past, and I've got to move on with my life. There's been a lot of surprise changes for all of us, and I can see a few more of them coming our way."

"Life's always got a surprise or two up its sleeve. Could even fit in a few extra if it's empty like my left one."

"Maybe I got some up my own sleeve, too, Pa."

The chirping of the peepers continued awhile without competition. Wordlessly, Pa stood like a statue, while Jem slowly rubbed his palms together.

"I suppose," he said softly, "it's best if I just tell you flat out, so here it is."

They stared into the darkness. The song of the peepers surrounded them for a minute that seemed as long as the rest of the night. Jem wouldn't have been surprised to see the gentle glow of dawn gradually revealing the lilac bushes at the edge of the yard. At last he spoke.

"Another hard part about getting home is that I've got to leave again right soon."

"That doesn't really surprise me." Pa sighed, sounding relieved. "It's springtime and the sap's rising. Ever since you told me about her, I figured you'd be off to Washington to see that pretty little girl you met in the hospital."

"That's one thing, Pa. I do want to do that."

"Of course you do. It's only natural. Visit Mrs. Dawson tomorrow and next day go over to John Nicholls's harness store and ask if someone can lend you a horse. Get an early start, and you'll easily make it before sunset. If she's all the girl you say she is, she'll be happy to see you, and in a few days you can come back for the barn raising. And later on, one fine day, if you're lucky, the two of you'll get married and you'll bring her back here to see that barn for herself. It's only natural."

"But that's not the whole of it, Pa. The other part is that I have to leave for a time. I have to visit with Sarah, and then I have to move on."

"Back here."

"No, Pa. Not here. I can't rightly say where. Could be anywhere. Could be Washington or maybe New York, more likely Chicago or even way out west. But it won't be here. Not for a time, anyway."

"Whee-ew!" whistled Pa, staring into the darkness. Slowly, he began to shake his head. Then he said "whew" again, more softly. "That sure is some surprise. After all we've been through, why would you want to go and do a thing like that?"

"It's hard to say."

"I should think so."

"Seems like saying it isn't as hard as explaining it," said Jem.

"If anybody's going to understand you, I will," said Pa as he sat down on the top step of the porch. "I've known you longer than you've known yourself, and now's a good time to explain."

"I started thinking about going away before Granddad died, but I told him I'd work the farm, so I had to give up on the idea. I didn't think much about it while I was in the Army, but in the hospital I had a whole lot of time for thinking, so when I got home, it felt like I hadn't made anything of myself after all. Maybe I was just a boy getting back to where I started, but I know, Pa, and you know it, too, I'm older and I've learned a few things. Seems like the country's changing fast, and I guess I want to get out and look around and see that change for myself. I love this place as much as you do, and I'll be back from time to time. Maybe for good, someday. Right now I want to go looking."

"The farming's changed, too, Jem-boy. We're short-handed here. That's not just a joke meaning I have but the one hand."

"I know, Pa. That's why I figure I'll stay here until we get a new barn raised and get things going again. I wouldn't leave you stuck with that big job all by yourself. Then there'll be boys coming back from the war looking for work sooner or later."

"Sooner, I would think. Last I heard, Grant had Lee just about whipped. But I thought you made a promise to Granddad?"

"He figured you were as good as dead when he asked me to promise. Now you're here, alive. We're living in a big, big country, and there's a lot going on in it besides farming. Now, you take Chicago. It's a regular city. Gaithersburg doesn't even have a train station, never mind a railroad line running through, but Chicago's got railroads in all directions. It's growing like a weed."

"You do remember, don't you, that the Baltimore and Ohio Railroad's going to build a branch from Laurel, near Washington, up to Frederick?"

"When is it coming?" asked Jem. "And if it does come, will it run through Gaithersburg?"

"Don't know and don't know," Pa replied wearily.

"Before the war there was the planning with the B and O board of directors and surveying the countryside for the best route. We thought we had it settled to come through Gaithersburg, but when the war came along, nothing was for sure and we put it all aside. Pretty soon things should work out."

"Well," said Jem, "I don't think I can wait for things to maybe work out. I've pretty much made up my mind."

"I can see that," Pa replied, "and that's all well and good, but it seems to me you've made up your mind to leave without knowing quite what it is you're looking for."

"I guess it seems foolish to you, Pa. I must look like some kind of jack-in-the-box. You see, the first time I left, I thought I knew exactly what I was looking for. But what I got into wasn't anywhere near what I expected. Hank and I learned to kill fellows just like us. That's not the same thing as picking off rats around the corncrib. Rebels aren't rats, they're people, but we've been killing thousands and thousands of them like they were vermin. And they're doing the same to us. That's too much death and destruction for just about any cause I can think of."

"I'd have to agree with you there, son, but for you and me it's over, and none of the past changes what we face right here."

"I think it does. Pa, I love you, but I have to disagree. For me the war has changed almost everything. Before I went away, I might have spent the rest of my life right here in Gaithersburg and never thought much about it. And I believe that would have been a very good life, especially working alongside you. Maybe someday I will settle down here, but I won't know about that until I go out and see what else is happening or about to happen in this country."

"And you figure Sarah will just wait for you while you do all this traveling?"

"It's a chance I have to take. Someday I hope she'll be happy for us to share a life together, but I have to look around first, and then I can come back to her. And maybe, maybe even back here."

"Well," said Pa, slowly, "I believe a man has to think for himself, and you have surely become a man, one who makes this father right proud. You've got plenty of thinking time to search out your own place in life, whatever it may be."

"Wherever it may be," added Jem.

About the Author

JOHN B. SEVERANCE is a former teacher and the author of several well-received biographies for young readers, including *Gandhi: Great Soul; Winston Churchill: Soldier, Statesman, Artist; Thomas Jefferson: Architect of Democracy;* and *Einstein, Visionary Scientist* (all Clarion).

On childhood visits to his father's hometown of Gaithersburg, Maryland, Mr. Severance often listened to older relatives talk of the Civil War as if it had been fought only a few weeks earlier. This family lore plus a bachelor's degree in history from Harvard have helped him create his first young adult historical novel. John B. Severance and his wife, Sylvia, live in Westerly, Rhode Island.